SHORT BREAK IN VENICE

By Peter Inchbald

SHORT BREAK IN VENICE
THE SWEET SHORT GRASS
TONDO FOR SHORT

SHORT BREAK IN VENICE

PETER INCHBALD

PUBLISHED FOR THE CRIME CLUB BY
DOUBLEDAY & COMPANY, INC.
GARDEN CITY, NEW YORK
1983

Library of Congress Cataloging in Publication Data

Inchbald, Peter.
Short break in Venice.

Sequel to: The sweet short grass.
I. Title.
PR6059.N3S5   1983   823'.914
ISBN 0-385-19090-5
Library of Congress Catalog Card Number 83–11528

First Edition in the United States of America

Copyright © 1983 by Peter Inchbald
All Rights Reserved
Printed in the United States of America

To
Juliet, Mary, and Terence
Salute

salute *nf* health, safety, salvation; **s.!** bless you!
alla s.! here's health!

COLLINS CONTEMPORARY ITALIAN DICTIONARY

CONTENTS

SHORT BREAK IN VENICE

CHAPTER 1

THE SILVER MAN

The last time he saw her had been in Vine Street police station, and afterwards she had gone back to her cell.

But here she was, skittering across the Piazzetta di San Marco like a thin, preoccupied red hen. She almost bumped into him.

"*Eoh!*" Her vowels could be that bit too upper class. "Eoh, I *beg* your pardon. Er—*scusi* . . . Why! It's Chief Inspector Corti!"

"Mrs. Silverman, isn't it? Let me introduce the wife."

"Pleased to meet you," said Teresa Corti.

"*How* d'ye do?" said Elsa Silverman. "You're not here on duty then, Chief Inspector?"

"Just a short break."

It was midmorning. The café tables on the Piazzetta, warmed by mild October sunshine, were filling up. Teresa said, "We were going to have coffee. Would you like to join us, Mrs. Silverman?"

"'Elsa,' please." Even her voice was like a hen's. "But how *sweet* of you. I'd be delighted."

Corti didn't mind. They had only held her for forty-eight hours. The crimes had been her husband's, not hers. A lifetime of bent art dealing, a ditto attempt to ruin Corti's career, and finally involvement in murder.

But Max had escaped to Brazil. Corti's eyes hardened. They were dark and usually gentle, in contrast to his broad, scarred, deadpan face. There had been nothing gentle about his relationship with Maxwell Silverman.

They picked their table and sat down. He asked Elsa, "Are you on holiday too?"

"No such luck. Business, I'm afraid. My Venetian branch."

He'd forgotten they had one. Franco Corti worked in the Art and Antiques Squad, but the only branch of Maxwell Silverman International he knew personally was the head-office gallery in Duke Street, St. James's. He thought there were six all told.

He said, "Not trouble, I hope?"

"My dear, so do I."

She needed to talk. She was so overstated, so defiant. Her cheeks, her lips, the short straight hair, the big sunglasses, were all in hot orangey shades. The brick-red shoes and slacks and complicated tan and white blouse, the mass of jewels and etceteras, must have cost a fortune. The antithesis of Teresa, compact in her black and grey, with only her wedding ring for ornament and no makeup on her dark, determined little face.

"You don't sound very sure," he said. "About trouble and that."

"It's *terribly* difficult, what with Max living abroad, and no proper arrangements . . . I'm divorcing him, naturally, and thank *God* there aren't any children, but the business . . . It belongs to both of us, you see, and *someone's* got to manage the European end. So when all this blew up . . . I mean *I* wasn't a business woman. I hadn't a *clue* how to cope. I've had a year of it by now and I've learnt a lot, but . . ."

A waiter was hovering. Corti ordered. Elsa said, "I didn't know you spoke Italian."

"Spoke nothing else till I was five." That was when he had first come to England.

"Eoh! You mean you . . . ?"

"Born in Florence." By then his father was a prisoner of war and on his way to England, where he had settled on release.

"But that's amazing! Then we're both immigrants."

"You're from . . . ?"

"Estonia. You probably haven't heard of it, but it *was* independent. My parents sent me out, poor darlings, before the Russians . . ."

He shivered mentally and nodded.

"And Mrs. Corti? You're . . . ?"

"Teresa. I'm a cockney. Born in Soho."

"She's an Eyetie, same as me," said Corti. "We're a pair of

Raddies." That was not a word Silverman International's customers would know, but Elsa did. He wondered about her early years in London. You've got guts, he thought. And the best of Estonian luck.

He said, "I don't think I've seen your Venice gallery. Where is it?"

"My dear, tucked *right* away, in the Dorsoduro—that's the patch round the Salute. Of course it *always* lost money, but then Max wasn't serious. All he wanted was expense-account trips to Venice. But in this day and age—I mean *I* can't afford to have assets lying idle. I'll show you what I've done, if you like. I'm going across in a minute. Why don't you both come too?"

He felt as if he owed her because of Vine Street, though it wasn't him who had put her there but the berk Hunt. He looked at Teresa. "Shall we?"

She looked doubtful. "Oh, come on," said Elsa. "The gondola's waiting."

Teresa clapped her hands and a cloud of pigeons took off. "Oh, *yes!* Can we, Franco? You *know* I want to go in a gondola. He won't let me, Elsa—you know what men are like. Everything's always too expensive . . ."

As a policeman he shouldn't accept favours, but what the hell? This was Venice. He raised his glass of grappa to Elsa. "*Salute.* Thanks. That would be very interesting."

Meeting her like that had touched dormant nerve endings. He sat quiet while she and Teresa talked, wondering if he would ever put her husband away.

It nagged him chronically like the nag of tight clothes. He unbuttoned his blazer, but it still caught under the arms. The only coat that had had room for his chest and shoulders without hanging like a deflated balloon had cost a fortune. Perhaps when his father's will was sorted out, if it ever was, he would order another suit like that.

Pie in the sky. He forced it out of his mind and concentrated on Venice.

Not many yards away its guardians surveyed it from their granite columns. The winged lion of St. Mark and his predecessor St. Theodore, who Corti had thought at first was St. George, with his foot on a small but venomous dragon. The tide was up and lapping on to the pavement, and the gondolas fringing the waterfront bobbed high among a thin forest of mooring posts. Across the *bacino* with its bustling launches, San Giorgio Maggiore, serene and Palladian, took the sun. To the right, the tall dome of Santa Maria della Salute marked the entrance of the Grand Canal.

He settled up, and they strolled towards the waterfront, known hereabouts as the Molo. He found it hard to dawdle. He was short in stature, and in London he walked everywhere, marching as stiff as a drill sergeant with long, vigorous strides. Teresa was no dawdler either, but Venice got hold of you. A few more days and they'd be as idle as everyone else.

He liked the sound track of the Molo. The seagulls, pigeons, powerboats. A vaporetto rumbling to its landing stage. The constant rainlike patter of feet on paving, the quiet babel of voices. Ahead, a fruity contralto was coming into focus. An Englishwoman in a poncho and a toreador-style hat with a wide flat brim, enlightening her special-interest tour—". . . the *doorstep* of Europe! On this spot for a thousand years strangers from the East first set foot on its soil. Here Marco Polo took ship for Cathay. Here . . ." A ship somewhere behind the Salute hooted her down.

For an instant her face registered irritation. It was full, with soft, rounded features and a good colour. Then she laughed like a girl, looked round, and caught Corti's eye. He couldn't help smiling back.

By the time she got going again he was out of earshot and Elsa was pointing out her gondola. "It's the key to the whole thing. I mean *access*. People *simply* didn't come, and if they did they couldn't find us, then all that scrumming for the vaporetto . . . But this way it's a treat. They just adore it. Oh, I know it costs the earth, but . . ."

He hoped she knew what she was doing. Her gondolier handed them aboard, and the long black asymmetric hull slid out into the *bacino*. A silver statuette stood fixed to the gunwale. It was male, naked, and familiar. Corti asked, "Michelangelo?"

"My silver man. I'm making him a sort of trademark. He's King David, you see, and we're Jewish, so . . ."

So she was a showman. "And you think that's done it? The gondola?"

"Oh, not just that. I'm trying to get publicity. And diversifying. Antiques, things for the tourists . . ."

"And how's it doing?"

"I simply can't be sure. I mean I daren't trust the figures. Don't think I'm accusing anybody, but . . . But how can you tell? You know the police were round? That's why I'm here, actually."

An inner voice whispered, Don't get involved. But he was involved with Maxwell Silverman regardless. The man had been an obsession.

"Stolen goods, Chief Inspector. They took some things away. My manager swears he bought them in good faith."

"Do you believe him?"

She shrugged. "He bought them in Milan. Says he had to pay cash, but . . . Well, in this business . . . I mean this is Italy, and people's attitudes . . . Max used to say if they paid all their taxes it'd be more than the national income." It didn't surprise him.

"Can you trust the accountants?" asked Teresa.

Elsa Silverman shrugged again and twiddled her scarf. Her nails were orange like her hair.

"I could run through your figures if you like. My parents have got this restaurant, in Soho actually. The Vaccarino, in Beak Street. Perhaps you know it. I've kept the books for years. Not personally any more, but I still look after the finances."

And the kitchen, Corti thought, and staff, premises, equipment. Not to mention the old folks. No wonder the kids and I . . . Run through the figures? An A & A wife? I'd be off the Squad in ten minutes flat.

He shook his head at her. "Darling . . ."

"Rats! Why shouldn't I? This isn't London, Franco—you're off your precious patch and I want something to *do*. Really, Mrs. Silverman, he is awful. What's right, what's wrong, can't do this, can't do that—I don't know how I stand it. And the children too —they get that sick of it. There'll be trouble one of these days, Franco Corti, and don't say I didn't warn you. Turning them into little revolutionaries, he is, except Gino and he was always Daddy's boy . . ."

He frowned at her. "Darling! Please."

With a lot of people the frown would have been conclusive. The glare under the thick, lowered eyebrows; the bristling hair, the long tight mouth, the squashed splayed nose that looked broken but wasn't. The scar cutting through his right nostril and down to the mouth. The short thick neck with its three-inch acid burn. The enormous shoulders . . .

The display of the fighting male, as effective against Teresa as a cricket bat against bullets.

"It's all very well for you . . ." She stopped. Elsa Silverman had coughed. He wished he could cough like that.

He took advantage of the silence. "I'm sorry about the stolen goods, Mrs. Silverman. I don't want to be inquisitive, but . . ."

"Of course. It was a mixed lot. Little things like miniatures, snuffboxes, netsukes. Small but quite valuable. Zani paid seventy million plus. Well, that's what's in the books—the ones he shows me. Max used to say that in Italy everyone keeps three sets, one for the tax man, one for the management, one for himself."

The money sounded astronomical till you worked it out, when it came to maybe thirty thousand pounds. She would want to sell for twice that.

"Did they say where the things were nicked?"

"My dear, from Pierscombe. Manfred Block's place."

Block was a solid West End dealer, though not one of the biggest; people said he was too honest. His ten-bedroomed weekend cottage had been burgled the previous month. It was obvious who had done it. A pair of brothers called Little, though no one could pin it on them; you never could. The Yard had come in only as a post office, sending out lists and descriptions via Interpol. He didn't think any information had come back. And now, of all people, the Italian police . . .

The gondola had nosed into a dark side canal, negotiated two corners with inches to spare, and nudged mooring posts topped with little silver men. The doorway could have belonged to a warehouse. Four steps up from the water and you were in the showroom. It had no display windows but otherwise there were a dozen like it in the streets around San Marco. Its manager was a smooth Venetian called Zani Gasparin, who talked English for the sake of his boss.

She introduced him simply as Signor Corti, which made sense in the circumstances, and he played in. Yes, he was in the art business, Yes, he was from Florence but based on London. Yes, he knew the London Silverman and had had dealings with Max.

Teresa's strong little hand squeezed his behind a showcase. Yes, Franco, it said. This is exciting! We're accomplices! Ah, Franco, what a man you are! Do let me see those books. Please.

Time wound itself back. When had he last seen her like this? This was the girl he had married, not the joyless workaholic he had had to drag to Venice. *Carissima*, his great fist whispered back. Anything you like, darling. It touched her thigh and he could have sworn her breathing quickened.

He saw what Elsa meant. There were pictures of course, and some decent furniture, but mostly it was small stuff, antique and modern, including a lot of glass. Things you could take home by air. He wished Teresa hadn't got involved.

But half an hour later all three were sitting down to lunch on the bank of the Grand Canal. The sun was warm and Corti had shed his blazer and his yellow and white silk tie. They ate seafood and a fish called "toad's tail"—grilled "on the irons"—and salad and cheese and fruit. The wine was cool and light, and by the time he'd drunk half the first litre himself and the second was on the table, he was thinking that Elsa was as charming as his wife. He was glad they got on so well. Perhaps Teresa didn't see her as a rival.

Or perhaps it was those account books. Next day was Saturday. Gasparin was off to Verona for a sale and would get back late, so Elsa could bring them to her hotel. Teresa could go through them there while Corti walked the city and studied its art, and they were both invited to dinner.

The Yard was a thousand miles away. Somewhere during the second litre he gave in.

"Super. Cipriani, then. You know how to get there?"

"Sorry, Elsa . . ."

"My dear, it's so *easy*. You must have seen their landing stage. On the Molo. If there's no launch, just pick up the phone."

"Right. And where does it take us?"

"The Giudecca, opposite San Giorgio." The Giudecca is the scimitar of island off the southern waterfront, and San Giorgio

Maggiore, if you want to be fanciful, is the blob dripping off its point. "Don't worry, my dear. The launch is free. Half seven then?"

He hadn't walked so much since he was on the beat, which meant eighteen years. He had seen Teresa on to the Cipriani launch and taken off. It had been a good day, he decided, waiting on the landing stage that evening, and in spite of Tintoretto. All those acres of brown theatrical arm waving. He'd had him up to there. Give me Florence, he thought. Maybe Papa was right and painting stopped with Leonardo. There's none here. Not what he'd have called painting.

But they do have buildings. The Salute drowsed, huge and floodlit, against the darkening sunset. Lights in their hundreds adorned the dusk. What a city, he thought. She's wearing her jewels. It's the perfect moment. Half an hour ago you wouldn't have noticed if the lights were on or off. Another half hour and you'll see nothing else.

They lay strung in long chains of white and orange. A few, on the boats, were red or green. Their reflections wriggled excitedly in the water. He felt tremors of excitement himself. All this; a posh dinner to come; a wife with honeymoon eyes. What more could you ask?

Posh was right. The comfort of the launch after the teeming vaporetti. Flunkeys helping you ashore. Awning. Garden. Flowers. Pomegranates among tiny yellow leaves. Tiny, soft-lit fountain. Quiet inside. Space. Not pompous. Elsa with Teresa at bar table, got up to kill and in mauve for heaven's sake, with ham frills at neck and wrists. Bar cosy, intimate, underplayed. Soft lights again. Sweet music—piano next door. He bought them all Campari and asked, "Well? Any joy?"

Teresa looked judicious and got rid of an olive stone. He hoped she wasn't outfaced in her sober clothes. She didn't look it.

"It's all right," she said. "I think Elsa will be happy with the year's trading. He may be taking a few perks, but why worry if he turns in figures like that?"

"And the other sets of books?"

"Why worry, Franco? These are the ones that affect Elsa. You account differently for management and for audit, even in the

U.K. Stocks, depreciation, things like that. There's nothing wrong, Franco. Honest."

"It's *such* a relief," said Elsa. "You've no idea. Oh! Look who's here!"

A fair-haired, muscular young man was walking towards her with open arms. She jumped up and kissed him effusively. "Darling! This is Chief Inspector and Mrs. Corti. Jeremy Block. Jeremy's Manfred's boy."

"Pierscombe," said Corti. "Stolen property. Right? Is this the first they've recovered?"

" 'Fraid so."

"Never mind," said Elsa. "It's nice for Manfred they've found *something*. You too, darling. You'll join us for dinner, won't you? Jeremy's a sweet boy and an old, old friend."

"I'd be delighted, honorary godmother."

"We don't have them, you see," said Elsa. "We'll have to become Christians, darling, then I can be a real one. Darling, you haven't said why you're here."

"They wanted someone to identify the things. I'm going to police headquarters on Monday. Don't tell me the Chief Inspector . . . ?"

Corti said, "Just a tourist." Like Teresa, beavering away at those books.

The dining room was Hollywood and disappointing, though the menu was all right. "Beautiful," he said, as the last of his *tagliolini verdi gratinati* followed the San Daniele ham. "All right darling?"

Teresa kissed the air in homage. "Ah, Franco, if we could afford the man-hours that went into this, the Trattoria . . ."

The Trattoria Vaccarino was all right but not in this league. He let Elsa fill his glass and actually smiled, dreaming of his *scampi Carlina* to come.

But the waiter came empty-handed. "Mrs. Silverman? Telephone, please."

The main course arrived. They talked desultorily, not liking to start till she returned, while Corti's gastric juices went mad. His scampi nestled plump and rosy on a bed of rice. The aroma . . .

"We should start," said Teresa. "The chef will be insulted." He should have thought of that himself.

One *scampo*, fit for the gods, one forkful of rice, ditto, and Elsa swept back, dodging urgently between the tables.

"Franco. Can you come? The Galleria . . ."

He swore inwardly in English, then Italian, and tried not to bark. "Yes?"

"My dear, broken into! Vandalised! Ripped apart! That was Zani. He's just got back and . . ."

He put down his fork and went.

CHAPTER 2

SQUADRISTI

He trotted behind her, still thinking of his dinner, through the *calli* of the Dorsoduro. The hotel launch had taken them to the Salute, and soon she plunged into a maze of alleys. Two minutes later they were lost.

"But I'm sure it was down here . . ." The *calle* they were in was three feet wide and stopped dead at a canal. For a moment he felt threatened, as if some monstrous engine would shut it on them like a vice. As if its air hadn't been changed for centuries and had gone foul. A lot of people must have got indigestion in Venice, hurrying from their dinners to a scene of violence. The bloodstained cambric, the discarded rapier, a waterlogged corpse . . .

"This *bloody* place," said Elsa. "Come on, back we go."

This time she got it right, and there was Gasparin wringing his hands on the doorstep. Corti left her with him and walked in.

Enough lights remained to show the devastation. It was like war. Nothing was standing—showcases were upended, furniture smashed, upholstery ripped. A pink and blue chandelier sprawled in fragments on the tiled floor. Beside it lay a gilt and carved chairleg. Eugh! What was that? He had trodden in it. The place stank.

He said, "Bastards!" And then for Gasparin's benefit, "*Uligani disgraziati!* Mind where you walk in there. Have you rung the police?"

The carabinieri were on their way. Corti hoped it would be all right. The Art and Antiques Squad often had business with Continental forces, and the Italians weren't the easiest. He'd had a taste himself, but that had been politics. Perhaps it was better with straight crime. Anyway it was none of his business.

"Sods," he said. "Made a proper job of it, didn't they? Better not touch anything."

"But *why*? I mean who on earth would want . . . ?" Elsa's voice was shaky, with a whine in it, and a lot less upper-class. "And at a time like this . . . I mean with Max . . . *Why*, Franco? Why?"

Drunks? Kids? He didn't think so. "Any ideas?" he asked Gasparin. "Any enemies? Anyone who might want you out of business?"

"No. Competitors, yes. All have competition, but to act like this . . ."

"Personal enemies? Enemies of your family?"

Gasparin shrugged a negative.

"Theft? Has anything gone?"

Another shrug. "How can I know? But I think perhaps not. Though there is one small thing. A wax maquette—maybe thirty centimetres. Some pretend is from the studio of Sansovino, but me, I think not. A soldier in armour. That, I do not see."

"Is it worth a lot?"

Gasparin pursed his lips and looked judicious. "To sell? Eight, ten millions. We have objects worth ten times that."

"That's funny," said Corti. "Ah. Here they are."

They were knocking on the canal-side doors. Gasparin picked his way across and opened them and gasped. "*Santa Maria!* Madam, your gondola . . . !"

Light poured in, dazzling him. He stumbled towards it and looked out. To either side the prow and sternpost leaned graciously away. Between them only the silver David broke the surface. Beyond, a launch was manoeuvring, floodlight ablaze. A policeman with a boathook was talking clipped, lisping Venetian to Gasparin. He could hardly understand a word.

The man in charge was a marshal or sergeant-major. Corti liked the way he worked: very straightforward and courteous and efficient. He let Gasparin do the talking and interpret for Elsa, but inevitably got questioned.

Name? Address? Occupation? Police officer? On holiday? The

marshal gave him an old-fashioned look and shook hands. Policemen mostly understood each other.

A voice from the landward door caught his ear. It had urgency. "*Maresciallo!* Look at this!"

He followed the marshal. The door had been open when he arrived. He stared at their graffiti for the first time. What they had sprayed was a yellow Star of David, and sprawled across it, black and malign as a tarantula on its prey, their trademark—a swastika.

Being a Raddie made you sensitive to racial aggro. He swore under his breath and looked again. The swastika had a ring for its centre. He hadn't seen one like that before. Nor had the marshal.

By now Teresa and Jeremy had arrived. Jeremy came over. "Have they any idea who did it?"

Corti pointed to the graffiti. "Political."

Jeremy looked at the swastika without expression, then swore comprehensively in a level, cultured voice.

"Sorry," said Corti. "I'm not with you."

"Pierscombe. The front door. That sign. Skinheads taking the piss, the police said. Skinheads my . . . God, what a mess. Poor Elsa."

"And Pierscombe? Didn't vandalise it, did they?"

"Didn't exactly tidy up, but nothing like this."

Hm. Same firm, different carry-on? Different individuals, perhaps. A swastika with a ring in the middle. Swastika was Nazi, a ring was what? A bond, a group? What else was round? The world. Storm Troopers International? Why not? England, Italy, it could crop up anywhere. Perhaps it had; it wasn't something A & A would hear about except that it was antiques that had gone from Pierscombe. *Canaglie!* He wondered if Special Branch had anything on them; they'd got quite excited about fascist internationals a year or two back. So had he. Bastards.

"Sorry," said Jeremy. "Did you say something?"

"No. Why?"

"You were sort of growling. I thought . . ."

"Just remembering something. Sorry."

The strain had caught up with Elsa. She looked an old woman, and Corti was glad she had young Block with her. But it was Teresa who did something about it.

"You look worn out, dear. You could do with a change of air. It's Sunday tomorrow. Why don't we all go to Torcello? I know Franco wants to see it, and they say it's ever so quiet. What do you think, Franco?"

"Great. Why not? What about you, Mr. Block?"

"My name's Jeremy. Yes, why not?"

"You should go," said Gasparin. "Is very pretty and very particular, and the mosaics are restored. Also you can get a very fine lunch."

Young Jeremy was a gentleman. "Splendid. The lunch is on me. Are you coming, Signor Gasparin?"

"Excuse me, but my family . . ."

"Fair enough. On the Molo, eleven o'clock, right?"

It was midnight before the marshal decided he had finished with them. It was not far to the Cortis' *pensione*. They walked there in silence, mourning their evening. He knew his wife too well to try to retrieve it. She would hate him to touch her now.

Next morning a gleaming launch awaited them by the notice advertising trips to Torcello. He didn't like to ask if it was specially hired, but they had it to themselves. They stood on the little bridge enjoying the weather and the spectacle. The graceful bridges, the back canals with washing strung from windows and rotting brickwork. Then out into the Lagoon, where lines of heavy timber tripods called *briccole* curved away to the horizon. Out past San Michele and its cypresses, past the Murano glassworks, into an empty horizontal world of water and sky. And every hundred yards the *briccole* marked the way, sometimes on both sides, sometimes only on one. Now and then you passed another launch or a noisy outboard dinghy or fishermen in a boat. In one place a man with a giant shrimping net waded a mile from land. He was barely knee-deep.

Corti watched a British Airways Trident take off from the airport and felt sad. Forty-eight hours and he would be taking off himself, heading for a London winter and the Yard. The Guv, the hours, the pressures. Personal hassles too, because his father's estate . . . He sighed.

The only landmark ahead was a plain, very high tower, still finger-sized, rising from a low streak of land. "Is that Torcello?" he asked Jeremy.

"Right. Shan't be long now."

Islands became more frequent; marshes surfaced. They passed the island town of Burano and coasted to a halt by trees and fields.

Ten minutes' walk by a rural canal brought them to the centre of the island. A voice he had heard on the Molo was briefing a knot of tourists. ". . . When Alfred burnt his cakes and Venice was largely swamp, Torcello was a city. The cathedral you see before you, or rather the first of its two predecessors on the site, was two hundred years old. Thirty thousand people lived here once . . ."

And now, a dozen houses, a little Byzantine church, this engine shed of a cathedral. And also the *locanda*, with its vineyard and its garden, where the food and the fact that Jeremy was paying restored Corti's faith in people.

It was over lunch that Jeremy announced out of the blue, "I rang the old feller this morning. I thought I'd better tell him about that swastika thing. We're not the only ones."

"Oh?" said Corti.

"Max in São Paulo, Köhn in Amsterdam."

Köhn was much respected, and the São Paulo gallery had been Maxwell Silverman International's big growth-point. It was there that Max had taken refuge with his manageress. And their child, so he couldn't be extradited. And Elsa had insisted it was the end of their marriage.

"When was that then?" he asked. "What did they do? Theft? Vandalism?"

"São Paulo was in August; they bust the place up and took the cash; rather a lot, apparently. Amsterdam was ten days ago. Nothing taken but a salesman got hurt."

"And those swastika things? With a hole in the middle?"

"I wouldn't know, but Father seemed to think there was a connection."

"When was Pierscombe?"

"Tenth of September."

It figured. Nothing stolen except from there, so no lists circulated. A & A wouldn't have heard about the others. He asked Elsa, "Did you know about São Paulo?"

She snapped, "Of course not," and looked up at him, eyes wide behind their lenses. "It's *horrid*, Franco, and I'm frightened. All

Jews. All dealers. Swastikas. I mean where's it going to stop? Has anyone *done* anything?"

Young Jeremy started to say something but changed his mind. It was quickly and lightly done, but there was something he'd thought better of telling them. Corti left it alone. Tomorrow it might matter; today all that mattered was lunch.

And Torcello. The cathedral was naked brick inside, except for some onyx panels in the apse and its three mosaics, of which the biggest was a vast Last Judgement and not his style.

He left the others admiring its pantomime demons and went outside, where fragments of carved masonry lay among rough-cut grass. The little Byzantine church stood open. He wandered in and felt a mood of particular sweetness. In its heyday the walls would have been sheathed in marble and mosaics would have glittered dark and golden overhead. It was as bare as the cathedral now, but in use. It had the look of a place that is loved.

The only person there was the lady guide, in a chinoiserie quilted jacket and no hat, but a lot of brown hair. She was standing alone with her eyes shut. He waited till they had opened, then asked what the church was called.

"Isn't she sweet? She's Santa Fosca." She spoke as if they were friends.

"It's a bit special, isn't it?"

Her face lit up. "Do you feel it? So many people don't seem able. Come and stand here." She moved aside. "No, come on—it won't hurt you."

Under the centre of what must have been planned as a dome a slab was let into the floor. He felt oddly reluctant to stand on it, and when he did nothing seemed to happen, but something must have, as if some force or aura or something was focused there. He stood for minutes with his eyes shut, letting it soak in, hardly noticing the tourists who came and went. He had never felt anything like it.

It was Elsa who broke the spell. "Here he is. Oh, what a *sweet* little church!"

"Elsa," he said, "come and stand here. It'll do you good."

They hadn't sat down to lunch till two, and had taken their time. Afterwards there were stalls of Burano lace to be inspected, and tea, coffee, or beer consumed at Elsa's expense. It was sunset when they boarded the launch.

The air and the Lagoon were still. No one felt like talking; even the engine sounded subdued. The sun, huge and crimson, rolled down behind the *terraferma* and points of sodium orange appeared on the *briccole*.

As they neared Venice the boat traffic increased. Two boys in a rubber outboard dinghy played surfing games on their bow wave. A speedboat overtook them a yard away and circled aggressively, destroying the calm, before snarling into the dusk. It was light enough for Corti to see the driver's face. He was young and pale, with short black hair and an excessively tidy beard. Something about the cut of him rang a bell, and as their eyes met, Corti could have sworn the man recognised him.

Was he something to do with the Yard? Who looked like that? Thousands. Who behaved aggressively? Villains. Young, aggressive, dark . . . ? Take away the beard and try again. The mouth had been red, a little girlish; the expression supercilious . . .

It clicked.

Karl Leonardo Owen Springer, alias Len Owen, of the smooth, crisp, slightly foreign voice: "I am a cocktail, Inspector, a miscegenation . . ." Half of him Roman, the rest, as far as Corti could remember, Sicilian, German, and Welsh. A vindictive bastard who had been a sculpture student in London and mixed up with some right-wing international mob that believed in cultural purity. Only one minor conviction in the U.K., for racial aggro, but wanted by A & A and Special Branch as well as the Italians, and, like Max Silverman, a refugee in South America.

Ridiculous. It *can't* be. Franco Corti, you're imagining things. And yet . . . That bother at the Silverman? Just his style. Hell, not just his: what about Mussolini's *squadristi* in their black, buttoned-up shirts? Any *squadrista* does things like that. But that swastika was accurately drawn. And the only thing missing was a sculpture.

If it was really Leo Springer he'd seen and Springer had nothing to do with the Venice job, the coincidence was of a class which didn't in his experience happen.

CHAPTER 3

UNSCHEDULED FLIGHT

"Scotland Yard? Detective Chief Superintendent Papworth, please. Hello. Is that you, Guv? Shorty here."

"What's up, lad? I thought you were in Italy."

"I am, but something's come up."

"Oh aye?"

Corti told him. The Guv had never seen Springer but knew his name, and remembered Max Silverman well. They hadn't taken to each other.

". . . So I thought, seeing as I'm here, I'd have a word with the carabinieri . . . It's a risk, mind; there's right-wingers among them, and you know the way it is in this country . . ."

"Can't say as I do, but happen I can guess."

"I don't see as we've much to lose. I think it's worth it. Personal contact can help a lot."

"If you say so. But don't go sticking your head into any more hornet's nests. It's bad for the Force."

"I'll keep my nose clean, Guv."

"You will, and that's a bloody order. Shorty, this Block chap's got some damned good info. First Brazil, then Holland. Any idea how he gets it?"

"Trade connections? News gets around, you know."

"Not to bloody us it doesn't. We've to work for it. Okay, lad. Keep me posted. Regards to the wife."

The next call was to Jeremy Block at the Cipriani. "You were going to see the carabinieri. I've been on the phone to my guv'nor. Would you mind if I came along?"

Jeremy wouldn't. In fact he was rather glad, if only because of the language. And in fact the officer who received them knew little English, so they spoke in Italian.

He was friendly though curious. "Scotland Yard? A colleague? You are welcome, Inspector. But you know, if you have business in Venice, should not your superiors have informed mine? Or perhaps they did and next year I shall be told."

"Not business, *capitano*, I am on leave. Mr. Block and I met by chance through a mutual acquaintance. And seeing that I had knowledge of the theft at his father's house . . . Also there are certain aspects . . ."

"Then you are doubly welcome. We shall talk about it in a minute. Meanwhile the signor Block . . ."

They had rapport over and above the normal police fellow feeling. Captain Montani was about his own age, with brown, humourous eyes in a workaday face, and beard shadow on his smooth jaw, and he wore his uniform like a necessary formality. He picked up the thread as soon as he had finished with Jeremy, who had identified the Pierscombe pieces, sworn to produce them to the courts if necessary, and signed a mountain of forms to prove it.

"And now, *ispettore*. Certain aspects?"

"You know of the *uliganismo* at the Galleria Silverman? Then you will be aware of the symbols found on the door."

"I had heard of the incident, but what is this about symbols?"

He explained, and then he explained about Pierscombe and the São Paulo Silverman and Köhn in Holland, and Manfred Block's opinion of them, and Max and Elsa Silverman, and Leo Springer.

"So what you are telling me is this: that fascist *squadristi* have attacked in various ways four art dealers in four countries and that all these dealers are Jewish. Also that this Springer, who is wanted for terrorist or other violent offences in England and Italy, may be one of these *squadristi*; that he may have been in South America at the time of the São Paulo incident and that you think you have seen him here."

"Correct. There was an international organisation in being two years ago. They had not agreed on a name but the Germans wanted—I can't pronounce it but . . ." He took out his pen and wrote on Captain Montani's note pad VATERLÄNDERBRÜDERSCHAFT.

"The Brotherhood of Fatherlands. You may remember an incident at the Museo Severini-Vasari in Florence . . ."

The Captain nodded, a little ruefully. "I can see why not all were told about this symbol. There are officers, shall we say, who might feel some sympathy for . . . *Capisce?*"

He only understood too well. "Springer and the director of the Severini-Vasari had got up some theory that art is local and ought to go back where it belongs. A lot of rubbish about mongrelisation. 'Cultural purity,' that was the phrase . . ."

"That would certainly be to the advantage of Italy. But you say this was two years ago. And since?"

"I am sorry, but . . . My department was only concerned by accident. C13 might know something—that's the antiterrorist mob. Or Special Branch, but they are a law unto themselves. I could probably find out, but . . ."

"But then it would have to go through Interpol, from London to Paris to Rome, and it would never come here at all, or if it did, I would not see it. All the same, Inspector, we should keep in touch. There could perhaps be things touching this English robbery or maybe Maxwell Silverman International as a whole, which might justify a phone call. Officer to officer, no? I call myself Giorgio. And you?"

"Franco—Frank. The police call me Shorty. Franco is best in Italian." Two years ago Frank was unthinkable; a year later it was in and Franco was out, and either way he'd have been all worked up about it. "*Va bene, Giorgio*—okay. Anything else?"

"I shall naturally do what I can to find Springer, but . . . If you had done that, would you remain in Venice?"

"He was here yesterday."

"If it was him. Is he mad enough?"

Corti shrugged. "We shall see. Meanwhile these things of Mr. Block's. Is it known how they came to be at the Silverman? I understand the manager bought them in Milan."

"Is true. From a certain Bullo. We do not suspect Gasparin."

"And Bullo?"

"Investigation continues. Our colleagues in Milan will report in due time and will act as if they have reason. They have the same photographs and descriptions of the goods as we. The property is not actually required any longer, so if the signor Block would care to take it back to England . . . When are you leaving?"

"Tomorrow," said Jeremy. So was Corti.

Giorgio Montani shook his head. "That may be a little difficult. Unless there is a miracle, the airport will be closed. The strike . . ."

"What strike?"

"The strike of ground staff and other categories. Have you not heard? Not seen a paper?"

He'd been too busy relaxing.

"All the big airports—Venice, Rome, Milan. All."

"And private flying?" Jeremy asked when Corti had interpreted.

"It could continue. It is only the international airports."

"Will Jesolo be open?"

"Why not?"

Corti asked, "Jesolo?"

"Near the Lido, between the lagoon and the sea," said Jeremy. "No problem. Rentawing. Air taxi. All lined up. So if you and your wife have to get home . . ."

"That's nice of you. Can we talk about it later?" He wasn't meant to accept favours, but he wasn't meant to be late either. First thing Wednesday or there'd be trouble.

Jeremy explained while they walked back to the Piazzetta, where Teresa should be waiting at the café.

"There's this little collection we bought in Padua. It's valuable, it's not bulky, and it's fragile—majolica, porcelain, some lovely old glass. Father's got a buyer coming over from the States, so he thought, seeing someone was going to have to come here anyway . . . Things can take such ages in transit, and however well they're packed . . . Anyway, here I am, the plane's there, and there's room. You'd be welcome."

"That's really nice of you. I'd like to accept, but I'll have to clear it with my Guv'nor."

He rang Chief Superintendent Papworth from his *pensione*, with Teresa grumbling over a wasted morning, and got grudging approval. "But you've to pay your way. Find out what refund you're entitled to and give to Block's. No mucking about, Shorty. Do it. And bring me the receipt."

It took the rest of the morning to find the airline and sort that out. They lunched outdoors by the Ponte di Rialto, spent the afternoon shopping and dined extravagantly, seeing they'd had two meals free, and Teresa went honeymoony again and this time nothing spoilt it. In the morning there was time for Santa Maria della Salute.

It towered above them, cold and aloof. It was the same inside. In a space that shape and that big, it was hard to see how it could be much else. "Like being inside an intellectual exercise," he said. "It's the outside that counts. Might as well look round now we're here."

One of the pictures in the sacristy was an icon of the Madonna. She came from an ancient, different Eastern world and was very strange. She sat red-robed against a ground of embossed sheet silver, the Child on her knee looking like a small and slightly worried clerk. Their crowns were goldsmith's work and jewelled. More jewels, and innumerable fine gold chains, hung across their painted chests from real shoulder clasps.

But what you looked at was the face, Asian-fine and African-dark, watching oblivious of the finery.

"She's like Sylvie," said Teresa. Their eldest daughter was fourteen.

"She is, except Sylvie's not so dark. And I'll tell you what else she reminds me of. Last Sunday. Remember Santa Fosca on Torcello? That place gave me a very funny feeling. It's an odd name, is that. I thought so at the time."

Fosca means sombre, dusky, dark.

". . . And now look at this. What on earth's she doing here?" The Black Madonna gave the place the thing it was lacking, the thing Santa Fosca had in such abundance. He remembered that the Salute was the city's offering to the Madonna for deliverance from plague. And that word *salute*, meaning both health and salvation . . . ?

He shrugged. "Makes you wonder, dunnit? Come on, darling; time we got back."

Earth and water swung, pitched like a roof, past the port wing tip. A slope, his senses insisted, defying reason; as flat as slate and patterned with tangled, writhing creeks. You couldn't tell if they

were full or dry. Or perhaps the whole surface was covered, like a
picture under glass. A tilted desolation, untouched by man, as flat
and strange and intricate as if God had gone abstract with a
paintbrush.

With no sensation of movement the pattern slewed and lev-
elled, and there was the city floating, sunlit and *serenissima*, like
the leaf of a gigantic water plant. The spire of San Giorgio Maggiore travelled the waterfront, pointing out the monuments. The
Doges' Palace, San Marco, the Salute . . .

Suddenly there was only sky. He shook the magic out of his
head and caught the eye of his wife, who sat facing him. "Sad?"

"No. Well, a little. For you, and for Elsa."

Elsa was sitting beside her with a few inches of gangway in between. She had done all she could in Venice, and now it would
be banks, accountants, lawyers, and then decision. Soldier on?
Pull out of Venice? Sack Gasparin whom the carabinieri had
grilled and let go, reckoning he'd bought the Pierscombe things
in good faith, or if he hadn't, they'd no evidence. London
wouldn't be easy for Elsa.

The plane hummed on, still climbing. Beside him across the
narrow gangway and, like him, facing astern, Jeremy Block was
deep in *Country Life*. He could hear monosyllables passing on
the curtained-off flight deck between the pilot and a taciturn man
called Meyer, who was some sort of purchasing agent for Block's
and acting as copilot.

This executive flying was okay. The Piper Cheyenne from Rentawing was hardly bigger inside than a large estate car but it had
room for your shoulders. He dozed off.

A movement and a change in the light woke him. Jeremy,
drawing his window blind to keep the sun out of Teresa's eyes. It
was low and striking right across the plane . . .

Sun? Ahead and to the right? At four in the afternoon? He
looked out, and below them lay the sea. He slipped cautiously
from his seat and went to the starboard window behind Elsa.
Below the sun a plain stretched away to far-off mountains dusted
with snow.

Back in his seat, he leant across and said very quietly,
"Jeremy."

"Huh?"

"Keep your voice down. Look at the geography and tell me what you think."

Jeremy half opened his blind, sat up, and whispered, "Good God!"

"He's taking us bloody south!"

"Too right he is. Damn! D'you know, it did just cross my mind . . ."

"Eh?"

"Last-minute switch. That pilot . . . Said the usual guy was sick and he'd been brought in at short notice. And I *thought* . . . How stupid can you get? Always play your hunches. Always. I know that, for heaven's sake, and then I don't do it. Look, I'll have a word with Meyer . . ."

"Meyer?"

Jeremy leant further and whispered in his ear. "Security." He tapped the copilot's shoulder. "What's going on?"

Meyer handed him his headset.

Corti edged forward and heard Jeremy say into the mike, "What the hell's all this?"

A pause, then, "Oh," in a voice that didn't sound good, and an unconvincing, "You're joking!"

The next thing he said was, "If you say so." He gave the headset back and asked sullenly, "Do you believe him?"

Meyer said, "No. But I could be wrong, couldn't I?"

Corti couldn't place his accent except that it was foreign. "Excuse me," he asked. "It's probably none of my business . . ."

"I'm not so sure about that," said Jeremy. "There's a bomb on board."

CHAPTER 4

BLOOD ABOUT

He shook his head awake and said, "What!"

"A bomb."

"He must get us down then. What's he playing at?" The flight deck curtain was drawn back now and the pilot was showing no interest.

Meyer said, "He is under orders. We are instructed to fly to Sicily at four thousand metres, refuel some place there, and continue south. If we turn back or descend, the bomb will be exploded by radio."

"South? From Sicily? Hell, that's North Africa." Corti searched his brain for crumbs of technology. The radio bit didn't ring true.

"Can they do it?" he asked Meyer. "I thought you had to be close—within a mile, say."

"I thought so too, but I can't be sure. Okay, I can use a radio but I am not an expert. Look, they can command a whole spacecraft from millions of miles. Why not one little relay in an aeroplane?"

The pilot had elected to notice them. "Me, I prefer to live," he said with a strong Italian accent. "Also I am captain of this aircraft. We cooperate."

"What language do these guys talk?" asked Corti.

"English," said Meyer. "Also Italian, but mostly English. You wanna hear?"

He nodded and put on the headset. "Hello. Anyone there?"

"You slimy bloody Jew," grated on his eardrums. "You've got your orders. Stop farting about and get on with it."

He clenched his teeth and counted ten before answering. Keep the guy talking, show sympathy, relate . . . "You've got me wrong. I'm not Jewish. Not that I'd have thought that would make any difference. I'm just a passenger."

"Tough shit then, Jew-lover. My heart's bleeding. Now get off the air."

"In a moment. But listen—how do we know this bomb's real? I know a bit about these things. You'll have a job to detonate it. Can you describe the technology?"

"You impudent swine!" That made him think he was talking to a foreigner. "I'll do better than that. I'll demonstrate it. I advise you to hold your nose."

There was a halfhearted pop, quite close, a stench of rotten eggs, a hubbub of exclamations.

"Enjoying it? Oh, I forgot—it won't make much difference with those Jews on board."

He was getting angry. This time he only counted to five. "Right. You know how to make bad smells. Now tell me where your stink bomb was, and when I've seen what set it off I might believe you about the other . . ."

His headset went dead.

He swore under his breath and heard the pilot say in Italian, "*Va bene.* You will not be overheard or interrupted further and your instructions will be followed."

The flex of his headset was trailing loose. He snapped, "What the hell are you playing at?"

"Don't shout at me. I am the captain. It is for me to speak with these people. I cannot permit a passenger to interfere."

Before he could answer, Elsa and Teresa were crowding forward, frightened and nauseated and asking questions. "What *is* it, Franco?"—"Where are we?"—"Why are we going this way?"— "It's poison gas, Elsa. I'm choking! . . ." If it had happened without warning he might have been equally off balance.

"Please," said the pilot. "Return to your seats. The plane is nose-heavy and losing height. This is urgent. I command you. Go."

"He's right," said Corti. "Sit down and I'll tell you. Some joker's let off a schoolboy stink bomb, that's all. Well, not quite all. Now don't go getting alarmed, but it seems . . ."

He broke it as gently as he could, leaving out the anti-Jewish bits, watching the panic level fluctuate behind Teresa's eyes. Watching Elsa's eyes too. With clear glass in her spectacles they were green. Perhaps he was kidding himself but he thought he could read things in them—her own and her people's memories, and resignation, sorrow, hate.

". . . I think they're bluffing," he said, pianissimo. "At least, I did till that . . . Fooff, it stinks!"

"Hold tight," said Jeremy. "So this is a demonstration. A demonstration of what? Radio? How do we know that? Why not a timing device?"

Elsa said, "What? To go off just when he said that? No, darling. Surely . . ."

"Are you sure? Clocks are pretty accurate these days. Or it could have bleeped on his radio when it was ready . . ."

"Sounds a bit farfetched to me," said Corti. "Would Meyer know?"

"I'll ask," said Jeremy. "Blimey, what a pong!"

"Hold it. Meyer's all right, I expect, but that other guy . . . I should keep your voice down."

"Too right I will." He squeezed past, crouching for lack of headroom, to where he could kneel and whisper to Meyer.

The consultation made the pilot restless. After a while he said, "Mr. Block, please return to your seat."

"Get stuffed," said Jeremy and went on talking.

The stink was weakening now, and Corti was nine-tenths sure. He whispered to Teresa, "I'm going to sort this lot out. You and Elsa stay where you are and if there's any aggro, lie down." He turned and knelt in his seat. It was back to back with the pilot's, with a vestigial partition between that got in the way, so he readjusted himself, crouching right foot in the gangway, left knee on the seat, head pressed against the ceiling. He could see the pilot now; he was nodding and making little responsive gestures as if instructions were coming over the air.

Corti braced himself, yanked at the pilot's headset, and had it roughly on himself in time to get a neck lock on. It wasn't much of a lock but it would hold for a few seconds. He shouted, "Meyer!" and hung on to his man and listened.

Reception was better. The voice was suave with very sharp consonants, the language Italian. ". . . Renzo? Renzo? Are you there? *Cosa c'è?* What's happening . . ."

"It's all right," he shouted to them all. "No bomb. It's this creep here. He let that thing off himself."

And then the pilot had wriggled free and pulled a gun and was fumbling to undo his harness so he could use it, and there was a bang and the safety harness came undone and the gun jerked out of the pilot's hand and he yelled and fell onto the control column, and the world zoomed and plunged like a roller coaster in a rough sea, and Corti felt sick and weightless and his ears hurt and Meyer was screaming at him to get that heap of garbage off the controls, and there was blood about and he was heaving and tugging at the pilot and Jeremy was helping . . .

And the wall slowly revolving and coming at them fast was the ground.

Then they had got the pilot right way up again and his control column moved in unison with Meyer's and the engine note changed and something was trying to push Corti through the floor and he was disoriented and afraid of passing out. But he hung on to the pilot till the sky went more or less where it should be and the world settled down.

And his heart was hammering his ribs till they hurt and his eardrums throbbed, and if he'd seen himself in a mirror, he'd have been horrified.

He could hold the pilot one-handed now. He used the other to pick up the headset and say, "Are you there?"

"Renzo . . . ?"

"He'll live, Sunshine. See you. Over and out."

"Okay," said Meyer. "Thanks. Have you got him? Where did you learn those locks?"

"Judo. Brown belt. Never quite made black. I'd better patch him up. Come on, you."

The pilot was nursing his right arm; then with a grunt he let it hang down and clutched his belly left-handed. Blood dribbled from his sleeve and onto the automatic lying where it had fallen on the floor. Corti wiped it on the carpet and looked it over. Walther PPK. He showed it to Meyer. "See that? Safety catch off. I believe the sod would have used it."

Meyer hissed at the pilot, "Would you?"

Corti felt him stiffen, then Meyer hit him backhanded on the mouth and shouted, "Answer, you bastard!"

"Stop that!" said Corti.

Meyer hit the pilot again.

He moved between them. "That's enough, Meyer. I'm a police officer and this aircraft's British. Do that again and I'll throw the book at you."

Meyer turned his head and glared. His eyes were pale grey and he wore metal-rimmed glasses. He was over forty and durable, with a weathered face and grizzled, inch-long hair. He stood six inches taller than Corti and weighed perhaps two stone less, which meant a hundred seventy-five pounds and five feet ten, so he was no chicken.

"Police?" he said. "Now you tell me. What police?"

Corti found his warrant card. Meyer's eyes looked down then, angrily, into his own. He started to speak, faltered, tried a smile.

"Okay. British territory if you say so. I don't believe you, not in Italian airspace, but okay, we play cricket. No cards, though; not in my outfit."

"What outfit's that then?"

Meyer lowered his voice. "Government service, amigo."

"Which government?"

"Confidential. You shouldn't find it hard to guess. Meyer's my real name. The first bit's Shimon."

Corti grunted. "Right, we've been introduced. Now then, this git here . . ." Jeremy was holding a revolver to the pilot's temple, and Corti was struggling to get the safety harness fastened so he couldn't fall forward again.

But the clasp was damaged. "That shot?" he asked. "Who was it?"

"Me," said Meyer. "Mr. Block has the gun now. I got my hands full."

Corti hadn't seen him hand it over. His hands had been full too. He turned back to the pilot, pale with shock, who was whispering, "The stomach. The arm and also the stomach."

Corti undid his clothes, ready for horrors, but there was only a bruise coming up below the navel, with the skin just broken. Also, held by the elastic of the man's underpants, one small bullet.

"That's it," he said. "No problem there. Saved by his seat belt." The clasp had taken the brunt, and the bullet must have been half-spent after hitting the gun arm. He ripped the sleeve away to expose a four-inch furrow running down from the elbow.

He grunted. "Not much wrong with you, mate. Dead lucky, you are . . ."

"Low-energy ammunition for aircraft work," said Meyer. "Hear that, punk? You're lucky; the man said so. Next time I'll make it soft-nosed and put some power behind it. Now sit up and stop snivelling. Mr. Corti—first aid kit. Here."

Corti lifted the pilot's wrist to get at the wound and the pilot gasped. "Ah! Is bad, sir. The bone . . ."

Corti saw that it was exposed where it lay close to the surface. Bruised if not cracked, and the joint not improved either. Painful. He dressed and bandaged it and turned to Meyer.

"Now then, Mr. Meyer, I've a question for you. We must have flown south from the word go. Half circled Venice, then turned right. I thought nothing of it. Well, air lanes and that; they don't always head straight where they're going, do they? But, looking back . . ."

Meyer nodded. "I tell you what happens. We fly round Venice so you can look at it, then these guys come on the air with this *fonfer* of fly south or else. So I think, Shimon Meyer, wait. Listen. Make your mind up slow. Don't alarm the passengers, not yet. I don't know you're police, I don't know about this detonating trick. So I play along, I think, I make plans."

"What plans?"

"To jump that guy if he's not on the level. That's a problem if you're flying a plane together. Specially a Spam can like this."

It was probably true, but what mattered now was getting down. The sun was astern and to the left and the mountains no more than an unevenness on the horizon. The coastline had gone hazy, and not far ahead it vanished under a thick white duvet that reminded Corti of the dressing on the pilot's arm.

"Back to Venice then?" he asked.

Meyer said, "Right."

"Look at that lot down there? That's not fog, is it?"

"Could be. I've been looking at it for ten minutes."

"What about Venice? Are you in radio contact?"

"Should be. Hold it. I'll—oh God! That dope—move him! Get him out of that seat!"

The pilot had dropped forward again. Corti hauled him upright before the plane was into its dive and half dragged, half walked him into the cabin. The plane was wavering, and in a moment there was another shout from Meyer. "She's all out of trim. Someone come forward quick!"

"Jeremy," said Corti, and Jeremy squeezed past and into the pilot's seat while Corti dropped the pilot, none too gently, into his. He turned to Teresa. "All right, darling? He's taking us back. Shouldn't be long now."

She said, "Oh, Franco!" in a strangled sort of voice and clung to him. He could feel her sobbing. "Franco, you were so brave!"

"How did you know?" said Elsa. "How did you know they were lying?"

"This git was so obviously on their side. And that stupid stink bomb . . ." You could still smell it. "And then when I grabbed his headset there was this guy calling him by name."

The pilot's eyes were open and showing interest. He prodded him with a foot. "Renzo? Renzo who?"

"Gobboni."

He switched to Italian. "Right then, Gobboni. Where's the regular pilot?"

"He is not hurt. He will be released."

"Oh, he will, will he? Who by? Who's behind this, eh?"

"*Prego*, I don't know. They don't say their names."

"And the big boss? What about him?"

"The *capoccia*? *Numero Uno*? Him we don't see, just *Numero Tre*."

"Number Three then, what's he like?"

"The face, I don't know. He wears a hood."

"Build?"

"*Così così*. Medium. Maybe lighter than that."

"Clothes?"

"Dark things. Black. Is very tidy."

"Voice?"

"On the radio. You heard it."

"Not enough. Is he Italian?"

A shrug; a grimace as if his arm felt it. "Maybe. The English boys say is not quite English. We say is not quite Italian. Maybe is both."

A tap on his shoulder broke the thread. Meyer.

"I'm in touch with Venice. The fog is bad but possible, visibility eight hundred metres. They will talk us down and we land at Tessera . . ."

"Tessera?"

"Marco Polo airport. At the end of the Lagoon. They open it for the emergency. But this talking down—I don't know. It's a lot of years since . . . Look, maybe on my pilot's certificate my government stretches a point or two. Okay, so I can fly a plane, but . . . What about this guy here?"

The pilot looked as promising as a sick ape. Corti said, "Well?"

Another shrug. Another grimace. Brown, wounded-animal eyes appealed for mercy, then closed to reopen altered, belonging to a man. "Why not? If Mr. Meyer can be ready to assist. How near are we?"

Meyer pointed offshore, where spits of land protruded from under the white pad. "That's the Po delta. Ten minutes?"

Gobboni said, "Okay. Fasten your seat belts, please," and changed places with Jeremy without help.

The sun was low now, and the mountains beneath it lost. Ahead, Corti could see distant foothills, and beyond them faint Alpine profiles turning gold. They were above the fog; it was impossible to tell how far. The engines were throttled back. Then wisps of cloud were whipping past, and in a moment they were in it and it turned grey and the engines sounded hushed.

Corti turned to Teresa. Their outward flight had been her first and she'd been anxious. "All right, love?"

No reaction. She had her eyes shut and seemed to be praying. He left her to it. Elsa was doing deep-breathing exercises and looking old. Jeremy sat looking tense, and all he could see of Meyer was his back. Gobboni's arm came out of its sling when it had to, and there was a lot of red on the dressing. He was talking constantly on the radio.

It was a long ten minutes. Flaps and undercarriage went down, the mist became murk, then without warning there were trees and houses just below, then marsh, water, lights flashing past, a tremendous jolt, another. "Bloody hell!" from Jeremy, a shout of pain and an obscenity about the Madonna from Gobboni, and they were down.

CHAPTER 5

THE NATURE OF COINCIDENCE

He leant against the rail of the carabinieri launch, taking it all in. The fog, thinner now and rosy, *fosca*, dusky under the sunset. The chains of orange lights like the Black Madonna's necklaces, curving into obscurity. Their reflections quivering in the Lagoon. The chunter of the engine, the bow wave smooth as Murano glass, the boil and tumble astern. And in the whole world nothing but the boat carrying them down its water lane in the quiet envelope of fog.

Fog? It smelt awful. This was the industrial smog from Mestre that was so lethal to Venice. He coughed and thought of joining the others in the cabin. They were all there except Gobboni, who had been hurried away in an ambulance launch. It would be warmer and less smelly inside, but . . .

But no. He wanted to think, to go through the last hours in his mind, assemble his facts, and see where they led him. The hijack attempt and Shimon Meyer led two ways. To the hijackers, who hadn't done well, and to their victims, who had, and who had known enough to have Meyer riding shotgun; and Meyer, unless he was lying, and why should he, worked for the Israelis.

Therefore someone was well informed, and someone had a hot line to Israel. Manfred Block? Not unless he was more than he seemed, which was a respected but still second-division dealer. All the same, the orchestrated aggravation was getting orchestrated response. Interesting, but hardly for the Art and Antiques Squad.

Except for the voice on the air. He couldn't be positive, because it was two years since he'd talked to him, and then only for a minute or two, but it was so like Leo Springer's. Which tended to confirm Springer as the speedboat maniac on the Lagoon. And Springer was definitely Art and Antiques business.

As for Pierscombe, the local force had its own A & A man, and taken by itself the case wasn't one for the Yard. But you couldn't take it by itself any longer, so that could change. He would have to talk to the Guv. He would have to in any case, because he could never get back on duty by morning.

The fog no longer glowed but hung mauve-brown and mysterious and faintly twinkling, giving the *briccole* lights little orange haloes. The first canal closed round them; its water was as black, its houses as squalid and decaying, as Victorian Manchester. They nosed for a while through slums and diminishing smog.

Suddenly, unexpectedly, they were out. Into a *bacino* jewelled with light, the great buildings floodlit, the haze violet and warm and no longer smelly. The Salute shone therapeutically ahead, half ghost, half substance, beaming out its message.

Deliverance. He stepped onto the threshold of Europe with his handkerchief to his face.

"Guv? Shorty here. I was afraid you'd have gone home. Bad news, I'm afraid. I shan't be able to make it for tomorrow."

"What d'you mean, shan't be able?" The voice was heavy with belligerence.

"This plane. We had an attempted hijack . . ."

"You never . . . ! Look here, Chief Inspector, if you're having me on . . ."

"I wish I was, Guv. It was rough on the wife, and I could have done without it myself. It'll be in the papers tomorrow."

"Oh aye? Let's hear your report then."

Corti told him. ". . . And I heard that geezer's voice. Can't be certain it was Springer, but . . . You told SB, did you? About the earlier incidents?"

"I told you I would, didn't I?"

"Yessir."

"Right then. So you're back in bloody Venice. And how long does Your Lordship intend to stop?"

"You'll have to ask the carabinieri. I can't get any sense out of

them; there's a right old flap on." It would be wrangling as much
as flapping. Questions of policy. Some officers would want vigorous action. Others, if Giorgio Montani was to be believed, would
move reluctantly, armed with labyrinthine and contradictory rule
books, while Springer pottered back to South America. He could
be halfway there already.

"Not much I can do, Guv. They're keeping our passports overnight. We're to report in the morning, and after that—I can't get
a straight answer. Whether it's just statements, or some sort of
hearing. I doubt if they know themselves."

"D'you know what you are, lad? You're accident-prone. You're
a bloody Jonah."

"Yessir. I'll tell the wife, sir. It'll cheer her up."

"That's enough. Just because you're on leave and . . ."

"Sorry, sir. Under a bit of stress, I'm afraid."

"So's all of us. You're not selling bloody ice creams, lad; you're
one of my officers and I'll thank you to act like one. Have we got
your phone number?"

"No, Guv. I've only just got back. I haven't had time to sort
out accommodation. I'll ring and leave word later. There's always
the Consulate, or this guy in the carabinieri, Captain Montani.
You want to make sure it's him." He hadn't contacted Giorgio
yet—you couldn't do everything at once.

"Montani? Got it. That's all then? Right, lad, you'll be wanting
to attend to your missus. Give her my regards."

"I will. And Guv, could someone give her parents the score?
Mr. and Mrs. Vaccarino, Trattoria Vaccarino, Beak Street. Or
better still, Mr. Dando, if he's there. He'll know how to break the
news. Speaks better English, too."

"Happen we could run to that."

"Thanks, Guv. Good night."

Their *pensione* hadn't relet their room, and fed them on cut-
tlefish stewed in their own ink with polenta—coarse, heavy food
that had Corti worried for his digestion. Then out in aid of the
occasion came a bottle of the *padrone*'s private and venerable
booze, distilled by his uncle, the real stuff from Bassano del
Grappa. A glass or two of that and you could digest shoe leather.
Being stuck in Venice began to be a bonus.

But not for Teresa, who had never left her children before. And now she never would again and that was final, and why he had to bring his rotten job on holiday was beyond her comprehension, and if only he'd gone into the art business with his father instead of this fixation about law and order, and he'd got to get her home tomorrow, and if he went on like this, he'd finish up an alcoholic. Hadn't he anything to say for himself, sitting there with a mouth like a rattrap, pouring grappa down it?

In the bedroom his own dams burst. He snapped, "Shut up! Can't you see I'm knackered?" and the emotion went to his throat again and he put his arms round her. And that was a breakthrough, because never in fifteen years had he stopped that flow. But here they were crying on each other's shoulders like the babes in the wood.

"Oh, Franco. Why do you always hold yourself in like that? It's like being married to a brick wall. Sometimes I think you're ashamed to be a man . . ."

"Not tonight, *carina*. Not now."

"Well, prove it then. Be one."

He did, and she decided not to go home after all.

Next morning the *padrone*, who was a thoughtful man, sent up all the papers he could lay his hands on. They were full of the skyjack story. The regular pilot had been found in a daze by the Trieste autostrada and was in hospital under sedation. About Corti speculation ran riot. He was from MI6 or maybe MI5. He was an SAS colonel. He was with the CIA or alternatively the KGB. And no one believed in his holiday: if a policeman got into a punch-up like this, there had to be a reason.

The media hadn't run him to earth, so he stayed indoors to conduct his affairs by telephone. First, the Consulate, which he had missed the previous evening through phoning Papworth. Then Giorgio Montani, who knew little more than was in the papers.

"So we have your passports? It is normal. The formalities should be completed today; meanwhile I shall inform myself of the particulars . . .

"A relationship with the thing of the Galleria Silverman? Ah.

Now in that matter I have news for you, or more precisely in the matter of São Paulo. A witness has presented herself."

"Oh? Do you think I would be permitted . . . ?"

"Why not? The signora Marsden. She is English but resides in Venice, Campo Santa Maria Formosa. You would like her phone number?"

He caught her just as she was going out for the day. Yes, of course they could meet. She would be happy to tell him what she knew. San Marco? The Loggetta? One o'clock? Splendid. And perhaps they could grab a bite of lunch.

The Loggetta at the foot of the Campanile, was as pink and white and luscious as icing sugar.

"Chief Inspector Corti?" The voice was familiar.

"Mrs. Marsden? But we've met before. Torcello, Santa Fosca, remember?"

"I do indeed. How very intriguing."

He introduced Teresa.

There was a superior pizza restaurant under the northern colonnade of St. Mark's Square. "So you live here?" he said while they waited for their food. "You must know Venice pretty well."

"I live with my subject all round me and some of the best research facilities in Europe."

"Then you don't just show tourists round?"

"Good heavens, no. I write books, I lecture . . ."

"Books? About art and that? Then . . . Your first name isn't Dido, is it?" Dido Marsden was an authority on all things Venetian, particularly art. "It's an honour to sit at table with you."

"I'm flattered. I'd no idea I was known to the police."

"Art and Antiques Squad, Mrs. Marsden; brought up in the studio. My father was a restorer."

"There you are. I said our meeting in Santa Fosca was intriguing. Do you believe in coincidences, Chief Inspector?"

"Can't say I've given it much thought."

"I collect them," she said in her rich, deep voice. "You should read Koestler. Conclusive, I would have thought, though outside my field. He's done all the statistics. These things are so much commoner than if they were pure chance."

Like Springer having nothing to do with the aggro at the Silverman?

Her eyes were brown and generous. She was a year or two short of middle age and her figure was generous too. As a girl she would have been the bouncy, cherry-ripe sort and he'd have been after her like a dog. She was pleasing now in her craft-shop clothes, and if he was more than just polite, he'd have trouble with Teresa.

"You're a policeman," she said. "Do you know what the Serenissima did with its criminals?"

"The Serenissima?" asked Teresa.

"The Most Serene Republic. If they weren't important enough to hang on the Molo, it took them out and drowned them. In the Lagoon behind San Giorgio Maggiore—a place called the Orfano Channel. The Canale Orfano. It was a capital offence to bathe there."

Teresa shuddered.

"There's more to Venice than canals and lovely old buildings, Mrs. Corti. As doubtless your husband knows. What was it you wanted to talk to me about, Chief Inspector?"

"Ah. The malicious damage at the Silverman. There are points of interest to us in London, and as the carabinieri mentioned that you'd come forward, I wonder . . ."

"Of course. Well, I saw it in the papers, naturally, and there was a picture of that swastika thing . . ."

He nodded. He had seen it as well as the original.

". . . So I felt I ought to tell them . . . You see, I was in America, oh, very recently, on a lecture tour. It included a couple of talks in Brazil. And when I was in São Paulo, the Silverman place there . . ."

He nodded again. "I know, I don't go much for coincidences either; not in this sort of caper."

"Yes, but did you know about the swastika? It was *exactly* the same, I promise you. The same man. The handwriting, if you know what I mean."

"I do. You can tell. Not always, but often enough."

"That's what I told the carabinieri. Of course Max was terribly cut up about it all."

"Max Silverman? You know him?"

"Not well. Isn't he under some sort of a cloud? I've always found him charming myself. Carmen too. Of course she's an absolute dazzler."

"Carmen?"

"His wife. She used to run the gallery for him."

"Not his wife, I think, but never mind. And how's our Max?"

"Not too brilliant. Says he's got a lot on his shoulders, but you may know more about that than I do. In Latin America one doesn't enquire too closely into one's friends' involvements."

He could have listed half a dozen major charges Max Silverman would face if he set foot in the United Kingdom, including those for offences against himself, Franco Corti. One of these days he was going to do friend Max.

And this, he thought angrily twenty-four hours later, could be sooner than he had expected. The airport strike was over. He was sitting in a scheduled Trident waiting for takeoff and for twenty minutes he had been paralysed, unable to make his mind up. Every instinct in him said, scrub the flight, get off the plane, get on with the action. But Teresa and the luggage were on board and it would mean hassles. With the airline, his boss, his wife, and Italian bureaucracy, and that was too much. And in the end he could be wrong. So he sat miserably, pondering the nature of coincidence, while they taxied and manoeuvred and ran up the engines and finally took off.

The paralysis had struck just after they said good-bye to Elsa, who had changed her mind and decided to stay a little longer. She had come to see them off, which was nice of her. Suspiciously nice, he realised now. She wasn't that close, even to Teresa.

Because the moment the check-in took their luggage, Elsa had kissed her hand to them and gone, and he had watched her idly as she walked away, and through the plate glass between the check-in area and the forecourt he had seen her greet a man. A large, slightly flat-footed man in a silver-grey suit, who flung his arms wide for her and she ducked in, pecked, and ducked out quick. It was only a glimpse, and from behind so he never saw the face, but even without the circumstances he would have been three-quarters sure, and the circumstances made it nine-tenths.

That was her husband, his enemy, Maxwell Silverman.

CHAPTER 6

FAIRY TALES

This time there was no circling the Lagoon but a left turn inland and foothills, then a lake to the right and the Alps.

It was half past three before he got to the Yard. The Guv was off sick: his health hadn't been too good and he was due to retire next year. So Corti had to report to Hunt. Detective Superintendent Hunt was the Guv's deputy. His first name was Neville, and he was efficiency-mad. He had done national service as an RAF officer and taken a senior command course at Bramshill; he wore a moustache that ran halfway round his face and thought he was God. He was much disliked.

"Ah, Corti. And what have you to say for yourself?"

He made his report formally, picking his words. ". . . So my assumption is, sir"—no one called Hunt "guv"—"my assumption is that Springer and his associates are mounting a systematic campaign against Jewish dealers. One, because they're Nazis and anti-Semitic. Two, because they're artistic nationalists, or Springer is, and the dealers operate internationally. Meyer's presence suggests that the dealers are banding together in self-defence with covert assistance from Israel, and I wouldn't expect the Israelis to defend passively. We could have a war on our hands, sir."

"Could we now? And why should A & A give a damn?"

"Two men wanted on A & A charges—Springer and Silverman. The link with Pierscombe. Block's role in setting up private armies . . ."

"Private armies? One security guard? Are you drunk?"

"No, sir."

"And even if you were right, how d'you know Block's behind it?"

"Instinct, sir. Something about his son's attitude? I was just extrapolating . . ."

"Then extrapolate yourself back to work. Investigating crime, not fairy tales. God knows we've enough on our plate. Anything else?"

"Yes, sir. Just in case it isn't a fairy tale, sir, I'm taking some precautions. There's a lot of targets in the U.K., and most are in London."

Hunt yapped, "Precautions?"

"Circulate the info, sir. And SB. Get in touch with Chief Superintendent Towler."

"Towler?"

"He took me to Rome two years ago. He was interested in Springer's mob."

"All right. If you must."

"And I want to go down to Pierscombe."

"Poor fellow. A bit tired after your holiday? A day in the country to recuperate?"

"Thank you, sir. I hate the country, sir, and I can do what I have to in a morning."

"You'd bloody well better, then. Very good, Corti. I'll see North Wessex are notified."

"Thank you, sir. And I'm putting the word around. All stations plus Interpol."

Silence.

"And Montani. I want to warn him about Silverman."

"Then do it and don't waste my time. Anything else?"

"No, sir." He got up and left.

In the Squad Office, Keith Billings caught his eye. "Afternoon, guv. Not too much excitement, I hope?"

"I'll live. How's Jackie and the baby?" Keith's wife had been on the Squad and like him a sergeant, till she got pregnant.

"Doesn't know what's hit her. Doing fine, actually."

"Give her my regards. And get me an appointment, will you? Chief Superintendent Towler, Special Branch. Say it's about Leo Springer."

"Right, guv. Will do."

Corti went into his office. He had it to himself now. The Squad's other chief inspector had retired and there was no sign of a replacement. Files covered half his desk a foot deep. He groaned, picked up the phone, and asked for the Venice carabinieri.

He barely had time to send for Springer's CRO file before he was through. He asked in Italian to speak to Captain Montani.

There was a very long wait before a voice came back, in barely recognisable English. "With who you wish speak?"

"Con il capitano Montani."

"One moment please."

Another wait while he visualised the ratepayers' money trickling down a small black hole, and at last a different voice, in marginally better English.

"You wish to speak with Captain Montani?"

"Sì."

"Who is speaking?"

"Capo ispettore Corti, Scotland Yard."

"One moment please."

Minutes later a third voice came on the line, in Italian this time. "Captain Montani is not at present available. He will call you back."

He left his number and hung up, asking himself what else he should have expected, then got down to his circular.

To   All Stations & Interpol (for circulation).

From   Art and Antiques Squad, New Scotland Yard.

Wanted for (1) homicide(?), and (2) robbery, London, Tues 10 Jun 1980 0200 hrs approx, (3) burglary, Pierscombe Manor, Nr. Chippenham, night 10/11 Sep 82, Karl Leonardo Owen Springer alias Len Owen. Born, UK. Date of birth, 3 Feb 49. Height 5 ft 9 ins. Build, slim. Colour of hair, black. Complexion pale. Smart appearance. Last seen wearing black slacks, black leather or similar jacket. Has also worn gold or gilt pendant of she-wolf suckling human twins (Romulus & Remus). Speaks fluent English & Italian, both with slight foreign accent. Last seen Venice. Belongs to international right-wing group . . .

He paused and crossed out "right-wing." Politics were taboo with Interpol.

. . . group titled "The Brotherhood of Fatherlands," suspected of causing extensive malicious damage and major theft of cash, Silverman International, fine art dealers, São Paulo, August '82; burglary at Pierscombe Manor (Mr. Manfred Block, A & A dealer, as above); malicious damage and GBH, Kunsthandel H. Köhn Maatschappij, Amsterdam, approx 13 Oct 82; severe malicious damage Galleria Silverman, Venice, 23 Oct 82. Premises attacked have been marked by aerosol with a black swastika with ring at centre, superimposed on yellow Star of David . . .

He smiled. "Right-wing" might be political but trademarks weren't, and if people chose to put political constructions on them that was their lookout.

. . . Likely to be planning further incidents, probably directed against fine art/antique dealers of Jewish origin. Any information to Art & Antiques Squad, New Scotland Yard. Message ends.
28 Oct 82, 1552 hrs.

That would go to every police station in London, every force in the U.K. and every country that belonged to Interpol. It was a pity he hadn't got a picture, but Springer hadn't served six months— hadn't been inside at all—so there wasn't one. He threw the draft into his out-tray, and as he did so the phone rang.

"Ah. Chief Inspector Corti. Shorty, isn't it? Towler here. Congratulations on the promotion if it's not too late." It was most of two years. "You wanted a word?"

"If you don't mind, guv."

"Come round to my house then." He gave the address. "About six. Okay?"

It gave him an hour and a half for desk work. In most of the files only one paper mattered, and by the time he got up he had shifted half a hundredweight. But not the frustration, because Giorgio hadn't rung back. There was no reason why he should have yet, but Corti was getting a nasty feeling he wouldn't.

Wheels within wheels, he said to himself, striding along Buckingham Palace Road; wagonload of sodding monkeys . . .

Towler lived in politicians' country, a quiet street behind Victoria Station. He looked younger than two years ago, but equally untidy. A doglike, pepper-and-salty man in a suit that needed pressing. Upstairs in his so-called cubbyhole the desk was like a rubbish tip, the chairs looked as if dogs slept on them, and it stank of tobacco. He'd forgotten Towler's pipe.

A file came out of a briefcase. "Now then, Master Springer. Mind if I smoke? Let's see—1978, inciting racial hatred, ABH, fined fifty quid plus six months suspended. 1980, art robbery, query homicide, you're on his tail. Has it away to Italy, then South America. Legman between Italy and England for this Vaterland mob."

"The real track record's in Italy, isn't it, guv? Terrorism, kidnapping, probably murder. I don't know if you've any recent information. We haven't. Not till now."

"Nothing on him personally and not much on his Brotherhood. They've been politicking, trying to set up a regular fascist international with them at the centre. On the whole the national parties don't trust them. They're not big enough, haven't got the personalities. At least they hadn't, but they seem to have a new broom at the top, and they just might be starting to get somewhere."

"Anything on the art front, sir?"

"No."

"Then I've something for you."

Pierscombe, Amsterdam, São Paulo, Venice; the charter plane, the glimpse of Silverman, if that was who it was. He passed on what he knew, finishing with the speedboat on the Lagoon, while Towler got stuck into his pipe. The room was soon a smoke box.

"That's it, sir. An organised campaign. It'll be Springer who's behind it, seeing as he was trained as an artist. Otherwise it might as well be bankers or professors of biochemistry. And the dealers are organised too, judging by Meyer. I don't know if your information . . . ?"

"It's them all right." It was Towler's first comment. "That swastika with a hole in it. Here . . . keep it."

The photograph was in colour. A door flanked by stone pilasters with a ravishing little Charles II canopy above. The door was panelled and of a rich plum colour except for the Star of David and the holed, evil swastika.

"Pierscombe?" Corti asked unnecessarily. "Have you got a magnifying glass, guv?"

Towler had. Under it the symbols were identical with those at the Galleria Silverman. He remembered Dido Marsden on handwriting. This was the same.

He said so to Towler, who grunted and went into an extended pipe ritual before answering. "Springer, eh? Who's handling it? North Wessex?"

"Right. They reckoned it was the Little boys but they'll never pin it on them. Typical Littles, except Charlie's usually tidier . . ."

"Littles? Charlie? Fill me in."

"Sorry, sir. Their file's part of the furniture at A & A. One of the old criminal families. Londoners, though Charlie's moved out now. Old-fashioned pro; knows his art and antiques, knows where to nick them, knows where to flog them. He's got records going back to his granddad. Filing cabinets of them. And very straight, if you know what I mean. That is, if he wasn't bent. Doesn't hold with violence of course. Quite an aristocrat, is Charlie, in his way."

"You said 'boys.' "

"There's Charlie and there's Roy. They're brothers. Roy cracks the safes. They haven't done time for twenty years; I doubt if they've been in court. They've a way of walking out of things. You can't help respecting them, somehow . . ."

Towler sucked at his pipe. "That sort don't spray things on doors."

"I know. And now as I've seen that photo . . . They must have taken Springer with them. And why they should lug a git like that around . . ."

"Rum."

"I can't see the Littles going political; not that way."

"So what are you doing about it?"

"I'll look into Pierscombe in more detail; follow up the Springer-Little connection. Have a talk with Charlie perhaps."

"Looks like we'd better pass the word. I'll telex Paris." Paris meant Interpol.

"I've done that, guv, and notified all stations at home. Would you like a copy?"

"I would. This is Special Branch business."

"Except both men are wanted by A & A, and surely SB isn't interested in Silverman."

"You're right. It's one for both of us. I'll have a word with your Guv'nor. Meanwhile you and I keep in touch, right?"

"Right, guv." It was as good as he would get. He couldn't mention his war against Silverman and his need to wage it himself. That glimpse at the airport had set off the old obsession. It was getting to the heartburn stage already, and soon it would be headaches and if he wasn't careful, doctors' surgeries and heart pills.

What you need, Franco Corti, he said to himself, marching homewards along the Mall; what you need is a safety valve. He was in Duke Street, close to the Silverman Gallery, before he allowed himself to understand his meaning. Franco Corti's safety valves were usually women.

And that was difficult. He wasn't one to go with tarts, and what with getting his father's place in Butter Court done up and moving in, and selling the Acton house, and the old man's will (which was a cosmic can of worms and he still wasn't sure if he was a rich man or a pauper)—what with all that, he'd behaved himself for a good year, and he'd lost touch with the talent.

Besides, there was Teresa, and Venice had been a second honeymoon, dammit, and when a man's just back from his honeymoon . . .

Something was happening to him. Middle age? Settling down? Accepting that he'd never be fully English or fully Italian? He was in Beak Street now, passing the Trattoria Vaccarino. He put his head round the door and called to the waiter who was laying up for dinner, "*La signora Teresa?*"

"Not here, *ispettore.*"

He hadn't thought she would be, on her first evening home. Three minutes later he was on his doorstep in Butter Court.

CHAPTER 7

LITTLE CROSSES

Maybe his children were a safety valve too, maybe they weren't, but they usually made him feel good. They were growing up and their welcome was less overwhelming than it would have been a few years earlier, when they would have been on him like a miniature rugby pack. It was only little Tony who kept that up. Gino, Sylvie, and Ches (short for Cesare) were into their teens, and Gracie, otherwise Graziella, who was not quite twelve, had always been the least demonstrative.

He stood in the narrow hallway with Tony hanging froglike from his neck and Gracie's arms round what she could get at of his waist. The older ones stood quiet. He remembered Teresa at a café table on the Piazzetta di San Marco—"Turning them into little revolutionaries, Mrs. Silverman . . ."

What had possessed her to say a thing like that? Women! He spread his arms wide. "Darlings! It's great to see you all. What's the news?"

He shepherded them gently up the brand new staircase while they told him.

"Dad," Gino said in his new deep voice that was stabilising fast. "Sylvie's got a feller."

It had happened. It was bound to. It was normal; it was hardly more than trivial, but he felt like a herd bull challenged by a rival. He tried not to let it show.

"Have you, darling?" he asked her. "What's his name?"

Sylvie didn't seem to have heard, and it was Ches who said with careful sophistication, "He's called Wali Mohammed, Dad, if that's of the slightest interest."

Vistas of trouble spread before him. Not that he was racist or anything—dammit, he was an immigrant himself!—but . . . But just about everything.

"That's great," he said. "Is he a nice boy? Of course he is. You must bring him round one evening."

But Sylvie wasn't there.

Teresa was, though, and Venice had done her that much good, it was unbelievable; and it was good to get back to her cooking and to solid Chianti from Uncle Paolo's vineyard after those thin Veneto wines. And Maxwell Silverman was forgotten and Wali Mohammed could wait; meanwhile Sylvie was his lovely daughter, and apart from her olive skin so like that Black Madonna it was ridiculous, and old enough for a glass of unwatered Chianti. It thawed her. When they kissed good-night he whispered, "It'll be all right, pussycat," and she blushed and ran off giggling.

Up at six; exercises, bath, shave. Coffee for himself and Teresa; his blazer and an extravagant Florentine tie for a bit of holiday atmosphere, and Franco Corti was ready to walk to work. Through the awakening West End with parking meters ten a penny, down Duke Street, past the Silverman, with its grille closed and a brand new silver David stencilled on the glass, across the dew-soaked autumn park, and into the Yard.

Paper, case dockets, decisions. He stayed with it till ten, then rang Venice.

"Captain Montani, please."

A pause, then, "*Pronto*. Montani."

"Giorgio! I am Franco . . ."

The line went dead.

Next time he was cut off at the word "Montani." The time after that he was told to wait, and there was a long delay before a voice came on the line that reminded him of the Guv in one of his moods.

It spoke Italian. "Who are you?"

Take care, said his instincts. He chose his words. "A colleague at Scotland Yard." They would know that already from the switchboard.

"Name?"

"Would you tell the captain it is Frank?"

A pause. He's wondering whether to press for the surname, Corti thought, and decided to hang up if he did. But his man must have shared his thinking and refrained. "Captain Montani has not come in this morning, but you can speak to me. I am his *capo*. What is the nature of your business?"

"It is not that important. Please accept my apologies for trespassing on your time."

That clinched it. "Has not come in" was a lie. It wasn't bad luck or inefficiency but obstruction that was shutting him out.

Why?

It could be a dozen things—personal quarrels, jealousy, administrative dogma, or empire building, or politics, or simple bloody-mindedness. It could even be to do with money, though he couldn't think how. And though Corti, brought up in Soho, wasn't strong on Italian accents, there was something about Giorgio's way of talking . . .

He had met carabinieri officers in Rome, and although they hadn't spoken alike, there was something obviously cultured about the way they talked. So maybe that came into it. The carabinieri weren't just policemen, they were the first regiment of the Italian army. So if Giorgio was, say, a promoted ranker among the counts, the *cavalieri*, the *marchesi* of the officers' mess . . . That could explain something too.

But explanations weren't the point. What mattered was getting through. Not that Giorgio would be more likely than any other officer to take an interest in Max Silverman—indeed, if there were anti-Semites around they could welcome the tip-off—but he'd rather deal with a neutral than a partisan, whether fascist or Jewish.

So, ways to Giorgio Montani? The official route was blocked. He needed a civilian contact in Venice.

He considered Bruce Zappaterra, coexecutor with him of his father's will. His people came from the Veneto: he might know someone. But Bruce was as bad as the rest of them and worse than most, and Bruce, who called himself an accountant but wasn't in the professional registers, liked cash.

Not him, definitely. Hector then? Hector Dando, bookkeeper and Lord High You-Name-It at the Trattoria Vaccarino, was also, to put it crudely, a spy. In Rome he had been an NCO in police records and had links with the Communists and the British Embassy. Then two years ago, blown and beaten up, he had surfaced in England with his wife and daughters and a note from Towler asking if the Trattoria could fix him a job, at Her Majesty's expense if you please. Apart from his Party card and some help against Silverman, that was as much as Corti knew.

Hector had contacts. His friends and relations were everywhere; there was sure to be someone in Venice. But that would be making a meal of it. And who could tell what axes Hector or his half-uncle or his second cousin's husband might want to grind?

Not Hector then, and certainly not Bruce. Who else?

Simple, wasn't it, when you used your loaf? Dido Marsden. She wouldn't be political, or not all'italiana, she would be in the phone book, and Giorgio had produced her himself. He told the switchboard to find her, and ten minutes later she was on the line.

"Mrs. Marsden? This is Chief Inspector Corti in London. I'm not disturbing you, am I?"

"Not in the slightest. I'm boring myself silly correcting proofs. Interruptions are a very welcome break. What can I do for you?"

"I think you know Captain Montani of the carabinieri. I wondered if you could give him a message. The thing is . . ." He told her of his unconfirmed sighting of Max Silverman and his difficulty in making contact.

"I understand perfectly, Chief Inspector. I do live here. Poor Max. He must be under a cloud indeed. Don't worry—I shan't try to shield him. If he's done wrong, he must take the consequences. I'll most certainly tell the captain."

"That's kind of you. And if you get the chance could you warn him about his own position? He might care to suggest some way I can reach him. Out of school, perhaps."

"I'll ask. I'll be terribly discreet, I promise. I expect this is all routine for you, but for a middle-aged lady scholar it's quite exciting."

He gave her his home phone number and rang off, feeling pleased with himself, till he remembered Teresa. He grunted, "Women!" and wrote a memo to Towler, who would want to know about the goings on in the carabinieri and his arrangements for keeping in touch. He'd want to know who he was using as go-between as well, but he wasn't going to. After that he rang the North Wessex Constabulary and arranged to go down next day, which was a Saturday, so the Blocks would be at Pierscombe.

The next call was to warn Teresa he'd be late. Like nine nights out of ten, he thought. Sodding awful job, a copper's; no wonder we all get divorced . . . When'll we get probate and tax clearance? If there's serious money coming, I could pack it in—set up on my own; dealer, private detective, security. Art game. Contacts galore. I could do really well . . . No good fantasising. Wouldn't want to let my mates down, or the Force. Or the public, come to that. I'm more use where I am . . . On the job, Franco. Get some paper moving . . .

Joint Sub-Committee on the Community Policing of Ethnic Minority Areas

Before submitting its second interim report, there are points on which the Sub-Committee feels it advisable to canvas the opinions of senior police officers. The appended questionnaire . . .

He drew his trusty ball-point and entered the fray.

That evening, ten minutes after opening time, he was in the saloon bar of the Grenadier at Farnesford, wondering over an evening paper and a Campari drowned in soda why he hated fumed oakco. The bar was still three-parts empty when Charlie Little strolled in and propped himself, carefully ignoring Corti, at the bar.

"Evening, sweetheart." The accent was gin-and-Jaguar belt. That nice Mr. Little in his City suit and Lloyds of London tie, relaxing after a hard day on the exchanges.

"Evening, Mr. Little. The usual?"

Charlie's usual was a large Chivas Regal. He arranged himself on his barstool and only then, with a start, condescended to see Corti.

"Why, hello, governor." The word sounded incongruous the way he spoke it. "What a small world. Fancy your popping in here! What are you drinking? Campari? Large Campari for the governor, darling."

"Not so much soda." Corti climbed on a stool and looked

Charlie Little in the eye for nearly a minute before speaking again.

"Business, Charlie."

"Isn't this a shade public?" The expression was confident, but Corti could imagine how he felt.

"Take a look at this."

Charlie Little glanced at the colour print of Pierscombe, shook his head, and said amicably, "Knickers."

"Not your style?"

"Absolutely not. That's nasty, that is. I don't go for that sort of thing."

"Someone does. I wonder who."

Charlie nodded gravely, and Corti, whose sensors were good ones, felt that he was less scared than at first, but embarrassed.

"Pierscombe Manor," he said. "Chippenham-Tetbury patch. You might know it."

"Should I? Is it open to the punters? Public, I should say. Can't think where one picks up these expressions."

"You don't like that sort of thing, do you? Swastikas and that."

"No, I don't."

He wasn't vehement but Corti believed him. "So what about a little cooperation? In confidence, mind. Just you and me. Because anyone as could do a thing like that could be a thief, and you know they've had burglars down there?"

"I might have seen something in the papers. Look, old man— er, governor, this really is a bit public . . ."

They couldn't have been heard; they had spoken quietly and stopped when the barmaid came near, but that wasn't what it was about. The message Corti was receiving read: I'd like to shop the bastard but what if he shops me back? We've got to talk about this.

"Okay," said Corti. "Where?"

"My place. Like a lift? The Roller's outside."

"I'll smoke my own, thanks. How's Roy?"

Charlie's brother was in rude health, the weather wouldn't last, the black man had got his fight sewn up and what the Government thought it was playing at . . . They drank up, not too hastily, and Corti followed Charlie's Rolls through the twilight— early, now summer time was over—between light Surrey woodlands punctuated by the driveways of imagined Tudorbethan keeps.

Charlie's house was early Victorian and white against the surrounding woods. It was light enough to see the slate roof, the delicate ironwork, the blood-red Virginia creeper kept well in its place. In the garden, as neat as any accountant's, fingers of cedar stroked a lawn broad enough for three church fêtes, and you could have parked a dozen Rollers on the gravel.

But the only vehicles there were two-wheeled. A pink and silver moped; a ditto pushbike thrown down on the grass. "Kids in good nick?" Corti asked.

"Don't know about good, but the nick's where young Wayne's headed if he doesn't watch out."

"Sorry to hear that. Is he still living at home?"

Charlie nodded ruefully. "He's out tonight, thank God, or I'd never have asked you round. Couldn't have heard each other speak, for a start. Sodding rock music, full blast, all hours of the day and night . . ."

"You want to discipline them, Charlie."

"Easier said than done. Mandy spoils him. Always has done."

Mandy, née Maud, had been around and getting blonder for fifteen years. The girls were hers, but what she liked best was boys. And gin, of course, and mink and diamonds and that. She must embarrass Charlie socially. He wondered what kept them together. Not long ago he'd wondered the same about himself and Teresa . . .

"We'll go in the conservatory. Campari, is it?"

"If you've got some."

"All mod cons, m'lud."

The conservatory was full of floral cast-iron capitals, plants that might have been nicked from Chelsea Flower Show, and deep wicker chairs. Somewhere in the house disco music was playing, but not loud. Charlie Little wheeled in his cocktail trolley. "Splash? Ice? Slice of orange? Happy days."

"*Salute*," said Corti. "Now then, Charlie. Pierscombe. Your style but not your style, right?"

"Off the record, are we, governor?"

"Cross my heart. You've not been charged, it won't be my fault if you are, and nothing's going to be taken down or used in evidence."

"Never trust a copper. That's what they tell you. But there's Old Bill and there's Old Bill. Stands to reason. You're in the form book, governor."

"It's mutual."

"Straight up then, governor?"

"Straight up, Charlie."

"So what can I do for you?"

"I name a name; you tell me yes or no. How's that for starters?"

"You're the bowler. Sling 'em along." The Littles were as fanatical about cricket as the Guv.

"Springer. Leo Springer. Does that say anything?"

"Sorry, squire, but quite frankly no."

"Len Owen, then. Same guy, different sticker. What about that?"

"Sorry."

"How about this, then? Slim, dark; proper young smart-arse. Early thirties, slight foreign accent. Sometimes wears a pendant . . ."

"Hairy great bitch with a pair of brats at the milk bar? Disgusting . . ."

"Name, Charlie?"

"Straight? We've got a deal?"

"On my life."

Charlie closed his eyes for a moment, opened them, and said, "Leppard. L-e-double-p. Owen Leppard. How's that?"

Corti raised a cricket umpire's finger. "Thanks."

"He'd chop my legs off, Franco."

"You'll be all right, Charlie. Stand on me."

"Bloody Nazi. One of those little crosses we have to . . ." Rock music, impossibly loud, obliterated his voice. Charlie jerked a thumb and bawled in Corti's ear, "Wayne! Jesus, he's been here all the time! If that young tearaway . . . Here—sod off! Scarper! Quick!"

"But why should young Leppard or whatever he calls himself . . . ?"

"On your bike, for Christ's sake! We'll talk later. I'll give you a bell at the Yard. This way out. Left round the corner of the house and drive off quietly. And no flaming lights, right? Ta-ta."

"Ta-ta," said Corti.

CHAPTER 8

FACES OF DEATH

Waste of time, he said to himself, struggling through the traffic towards the M3. What had he learnt? That Springer called himself Leppard. Big deal. That Springer meant something to Charlie Little, which was obvious anyway, and that Charlie was frightened of his son, which was irrelevant. Still, at least he'd be home by eight. By the time he edged onto the motorway his mind had filled up with his own affairs.

It was more than a year since his father's death, and probate seemed as distant as ever. The trouble was old Papa himself, cunning, wary, secretive; a craftsman who could turn a blackened daub into an old master; a dealer who after thirty-five years in Soho could hardly speak English; a father who had brought up young Franco single-handed from the age of five. Franco's inheritance was the studio building in Butter Court, a remarkable collection of pictures, fifty thousand pounds in tattered banknotes, an assortment of bank deposits, IOUs and property shares, and a mountain of assessments, valuations, countervaluations, demands, questions, explanations, protestations, evasions, threats, and even one receipt, constituting his relationship with the tax man.

No accounts, of course; nothing like that. Bruce Zappaterra, his so-called accountant, must have dreamed something up, but he wasn't showing it to his coexecutor. So the argy-bargy dragged on. Corti had insisted on his own lawyer, which had upset Bruce. Interesting, he thought, if it wasn't so hairy. In Italy they keep three sets of books; in London the old git, God rest him, kept none at all. And Zappaterra rules, okay.

And sure enough, when he got home there was a message from him. Could Corti come to his office tomorrow morning?

He rang back. "Sorry, Bruce, I'll be out of town. Got to go down to the West Country on a case."

"You work too hard. Your first weekend at home you should spend with your family."

Zappaterra's voice was soft and very persuasive. He thought, Don't you lecture me on what I should and shouldn't do, and said, "I thought you wanted me to spend it on the will."

"Half an hour, Franco, no more. Just a few papers to sign . . ."

"Has John seen them?" John Bennett was his solicitor.

"Those that matter, naturally."

"Hadn't he better see the lot?"

The answer was delicately evasive; and when Bruce, to his great regret, couldn't fit the signing ceremony in on Sunday, Corti wasn't surprised. Better pin him down, he thought, and fixed it for lunchtime Monday.

But first, Pierscombe. He'd kept the pool car he'd taken to Surrey overnight, and by half past eight he was on the M4, with the early sun behind him gilding a landscape gold already with autumn and silver with hoarfrost. Not long after ten he pulled up at the station where he was meeting the North Wessex A & A man.

He was called Sergeant Hopkins and wore a checked tweed jacket the colour of ripe manure. They went through the case docket over coffee in an empty teashop. Statements from Manfred, Mrs. Manfred, and Jeremy Block, from the gardener, his wife, some cottagers. Photographs. Reports from the CID sergeant who had handed over to Hopkins. Ditto from Forensic. A list of the stolen property—the one the Yard had put out through Interpol.

"The Littles." Corti closed the file and handed it to the sergeant. "That's them, all right, except the swastika and the mess. Forensic and fingerprint evidence nil, for practical purposes, so we're down to the statements."

"That's it, sir."

The job had been done around two on a Saturday morning, which showed the quality of the planning, because it was the one time in the week when the house would be empty but a car arriving in the small hours would be taken for granted. Young Jeremy often came down late on a Friday night, and two o'clock was nothing abnormal.

But on that particular Friday, Jeremy had an overnight guest in London and wasn't due at Pierscombe till next morning. The Littles would have made it their business to know that.

He riffled through the file. "Method of entry then. Alarms. Switched off, eh? Control box in an unlocked garage?"

"A lot of country people don't bother. And it wasn't as if there was any cars in there. Not as Mr. Block saw it that way. It was Frith left it open, and a proper old rollocking he got, I can tell you." Frith was the gardener.

Corti nodded. "Then glass cutter, sash window—locked, but they'd their own key . . ."

"Standard pattern, sir."

"And they're in. Including Chummy with the aerosol can."

"How's that, sir?"

"Left it in a mess, didn't they? Charlie and Roy never made a mess in their lives. Tidiest villains in the business."

"They could have done it to confuse us."

Corti shook his head. "I know them, you know. I was talking to Charlie only last night . . ."

"Were you, by God?"

". . . And he as good as told me they'd had company. No don't get excited, Sergeant. I shan't be able to nick him. But . . ." Corti explained about Leo Springer, alias Owen Leppard, and the sighting in Venice. "So that's the big one. The Littles may be thieves but they're not killers, and this boyo is. SB don't fancy him a lot, either."

"What were they doing then, working with a man like that?"

"That's the problem, isn't it? Now then, the bunce. Could they have got it into a suitcase?"

"That's what we reckoned, sir."

"M4, Heathrow, the Continent. It'll have been airborne before daylight."

"Or Bristol, sir, or Southampton. There's plenty of ways."

"Heathrow, Sergeant. Speed. That's how those boys work. It could have been anywhere in Europe before it was even missed. Milan, most likely. What time did Mrs. Frith . . . ?" She had been the first on the scene.

"She phoned in at 0933."

"It could have been to Italy and back by then. What time are we due at Pierscombe?"

"Eleven-thirty, sir. We ought to be on our way."

The manor basked, strong and grey and mellow, at the foot of a small coombe flanked by autumn woodlands. Across the lane, a horse leaned elegantly on a gate, while three cherished-looking stone cottages sunbathed just beyond. Eternal England—the scent of new-mown hay, slow dance of the seasons, hereditary yokels "zurr"-ing hereditary squires . . .

Sergeant Hopkins, plus the pong that struck as they drove up, gave a different picture. The pong was silage, the cottagers commuted to Bristol, the gardener, axed by the Birmingham Parks Department, lived in a council house, and Manfred Block had bought the place from a disc jockey.

Corti sighed. He drove between sumptuous wrought-iron gates and half circled an oval lawn with a fountain and four scarlet maples. The gravel was clean and even. The stone canopy swashbuckled over the purple, freshly painted door. It was Jeremy who let them in.

The hall smelt of flowers and beeswax. Classic English Imperial, he said to himself, taking in the parquet and brassware and Eastern rugs and stuffed animal heads. Fancy using dead creatures for decor. The style carried through into Manfred Block's study, which Jeremy called the library, but the theme changed to antique firearms and the smell to leather and cigars.

"Oh," said Jeremy. "I thought he was in here. Down, Pongo!" Pongo was an overweight and evidently oversexed spaniel. "He's telling us the boss is on his way."

Corti hadn't met Manfred Block before, though he had seen him around. A stocky, lion-headed man in his early fifties, wearing the remnants of a hairy tweed coat over a sea-blue open-necked shirt, grey shapeless trousers with wilting turn-ups, and clumping rustic shoes. He held out an incongruously soft hand. "How d'you do, Chief Inspector. What can I do for you? Down, Pongo! Good morning, Sergeant Hopkins." Traces of a foreign accent clung to his words.

"Just one or two points, sir. You realise this is the sergeant's case, but in view of certain unusual features . . ."

"Naturally. Do sit down." Chairs were in place round a desk like a boardroom table. "Sherry? Whisky and soda? Coffee?"

Corti declined and took a chair beside Jeremy. "Thank you, sir. I believe you mentioned to your son that one or two similar incidents had occurred abroad."

"You saw one yourself. That was Max's second; then there was Harry Köhn."

"What made you think they were connected with the break-in here, Mr. Block?"

"Graffiti. These gentlemen sign their work."

Corti nodded. "I'm surprised you should know about it. We certainly didn't. In fact, if your son hadn't mentioned it in Venice, we mightn't have heard of these incidents at all. Can I ask how you came by your information?"

A shrug. "Our stock-in-trade, Chief Inspector. In our business, news travels fast."

"Grapevine, eh?"

"I dislike the word, but . . . Pongo! Go and lie down . . ." Why that moment? The dog had been sitting quietly with its head on his knee.

"Grapevine, Mr. Block?"

"What else?"

"Could you be more specific? It could help if you told me who."

"Ah. Now you're asking. One sees so many people, and it must be two months now . . ."

"Since the São Paulo incident? August, wasn't it?"

"So I believe."

"But what about Köhn's? Not much more than a fortnight. Did you hear about both from the same source?"

"Harry Köhn? He told me himself; we often do business together."

"He handles the odd transaction for us in Benelux," said Jeremy. "It's reciprocal."

It was perfectly straightforward, perfectly consistent, but . . . Jeremy, for example, on Torcello, over Sunday lunch in the garden (was it only last Sunday?) when he'd told them about São Paulo and Amsterdam changed his mind about telling them something else. And now his father, using the dog to win thinking time . . . So the Blocks had their grapevine. Fair enough. But was it just commercial? And where did it run? Brazil, yes. Holland, yes. Israel?

He wouldn't find out by going on about sources. He switched to the Rentawing Cheyenne.

"Motive, Mr. Block. You'd had your allocation of aggro—property stolen, premises defaced. So why try and hijack the plane? The carabinieri are investigating, of course, but I'd like to hear your own ideas."

"We have asked ourselves many times. The possibilities appear to be theft, kidnapping, or simple spite. As to the first, the cargo was insured for six figures. As to the second, the target, if kidnap was intended, must have been my son, because the other passengers were included only at the last minute. And as for spite, it could have been engendered by the fact that we had recovered our property."

That made sense as far as it went, which was not very far. Corti said, "More than spite, I think. Don't you?"

"I expect so."

"Theft? Why you twice over? Why not spread it around a bit?"

The shoulders rose, disturbing the lion's mane; the palms spread in a gesture suddenly un-English. The eyes were blue like Jeremy's and fierce.

"So we're down to kidnap. Okay, but why your son? Why not someone else's?"

"How should I know?"

"Meyer? Your friend Meyer?"

"What about him? If you're carrying half a million's worth of highly stealable goods, a guard is only common prudence."

"What firm is he from?"

"Some agency. I think Rentawing produced him."

"Not the Israelis, Mr. Block? Shin Beth, perhaps, or Mossad?"

"Oh. It's like that, is it? And your own firm, as you call it? Special Branch?"

"No. But they're interested."

"Chief Inspector, nothing has been done, or will be, that infringes the laws of England. You have my word for that." When Manfred Block gave his word you believed him.

"Then you can talk freely, sir?"

"I could, indeed I would if I was a free agent, but I am not. I have given my word. Certain matters are confidential and must remain so."

Corti thought for a moment and decided to come into the open. The hunch he'd tried on Hunt, and got told to extrapolate himself, was legitimate deduction now. He'd asked Block why he was being picked on and Block, who was clever, had no better answer than spite. He'd pressed further and Block had played stumm. He said, "Mr. Block, you're a target for terrorists. Agreed?"

"Not disagreed, Chief Inspector."

"And the best reason you can give me is spite? No, sir. I think it's because a war's brewing up and you're right in the centre. I think you're the one with the hot line to Israel. For all I know you're the commander-in-chief. Do you want to comment?"

"No."

"Three points then, sir. One, private wars are not encouraged in Britain. Two, your life, and also your family, may well be in danger. Three, your best protection is the law. The police, Mr. Block."

"I wouldn't dispute any of that, but I have told you, I am not a free agent."

They fenced a little longer without result. Corti switched again: "All right, Mr. Block. You're not in a position to discuss your friends. I'll accept that for the present. But what about your enemies? Haven't we a mutual interest?"

"What are you thinking of?"

"Information."

"An exchange? I can see no objection to that."

"I wasn't thinking of an exchange, Mr. Block."

"Chief Inspector, we are talking business, and in business we don't give something for nothing."

"Nothing, sir? I wouldn't call the Metropolitan Police nothing."

"Touché." The fencing began again, and lasted, with no more hits, till lunch.

"Well, Sarge, what do you reckon?" The sound of the pool car's wheels changed as Corti turned into the lane. The waft of silage on top of a long and excellent meal made him queasy.

"I reckon you've got it right, sir. He doesn't seem to be lying; doesn't seem to mind you knowing what he's up to. Got it all sussed out, hasn't he? Doesn't need you and me. Got nothing against us, mind, but he doesn't think he needs us."

"Let's hope he's right; and if he's got to fight his sodding war let's hope he fights it somewhere else. We don't want it here."

It was ten minutes to the local nick. Sergeant Hopkins said, "Right, sir. I'm glad you came. I'll keep you posted."

"I'll just come in and use the toilet."

And that was significant, because otherwise he wouldn't have got the message till London. A & A had phoned North Wessex, North Wessex had phoned the station. The slip read, *Sir Charles Little would be obliged if you would call at his home on your way back.*

You had to laugh. In the car Corti got out his maps. An hour and a half later he drove up to Charlie Little's front door.

He could hear the stereo before he switched off his engine. He rang but no one answered. It wasn't surprising—the bell wouldn't stand a chance. Nor did hammering.

Now what? Two and two were coming together in his head. The noise meant young Wayne, Charlie's message meant no young Wayne, and they added up to something wrong.

He stood for a moment wondering what to do, and almost without thinking tried the door. It opened, to his surprise. He walked in.

The rock band, fortissimo fortissimo, was bashing out crude, aggressive stuff. Corti banged on doors, opened them, looked into rooms where Charlie's and his woman's tastes clashed visibly—his leaning to oak and antique silver, hers to pink wrought iron and life-sized cuddly toys. How did they stand each other?

In the conservatory, Mandy had less scope, except for some pot plants in one corner that looked like plastic triffids. And when you went to get a closer look, you saw that what you'd thought might be croquet things or something under a dust sheet behind them were nothing of the sort.

They were Charlie.

Minutes later he recovered himself enough to drop the cloth back on the mauve-white, repulsive face. It lay on its side half upside down, grotesque from the diagonal sag of the features. It was clean, but there was blood, still not dry, underneath.

The music raved and pounded. Instinct and duty in unison said, *Get out!* Corti got.

He dialled 999 from a call box and was told, like any citizen, to stay put. Half an hour later, having phoned Hunt from Farnesford police station, he signed his statement, and left. The interview had been correct but distant. Finding a freshly killed man made you automatically a suspect. It would have been the same for the Home Secretary himself.

He drove to the Yard ultracarefully, knowing his nerves were shot about, with his head full not of Charlie Little's dead face but of his father's, and the memory racking him. He reported to Hunt, who had waited in for him, and got up to go home.

The telephone caught him leaving. "Mr. Corti? This is Dido Marsden, in Venice."

CHAPTER 9

SIGNOR ARGENTINO

When he telephoned from London to recruit her she had got quite excited. She found him interesting and not unattractive, though a lot of women wouldn't agree. The complete opposite of Aidan, who had been thin, fair, wet, intellectual-tweedy, and obtuse.

It was two years since their divorce and she was beginning to react to men again. She told herself not to be silly. It would be fun working with him, but he was married and a thousand miles away. She put the proofs of her article aside to search the telephone directory and dialled the carabinieri.

Her answer was the same as his: "Captain Montani is out; I am his *capo*; can I take a message; who are you?" She made her excuses and rang off, still incognito, wondering if her accent had been spotted. Probably not; it was pretty good by now and she hadn't spoken much. If there was an intrigue in progress, which she wasn't convinced there was, and it was directed against the captain's lines of communication with Scotland Yard, it might help if she wasn't too obviously English.

That was it for the present. Deadlines were deadlines. She turned to her swatch of galleys. Forty minutes later the proofs were in the post. She had time for an hour in the Cini library before lunch.

She looked out at the weather. It was fine, with little puffs of cloud, and the *campo* with its market stalls was full of colour. The flower shop overflowed onto the pavement. A few tourists picked over the merchandise or strolled on their way to San Zanipólo and the Colleoni statue, but mostly the quarter was busy with its own affairs. Dido put on her hat and a light cloak, collected the shoulder bag that doubled as her briefcase, and went out into the sun.

The walk was familiar. Through narrow, confusing *calli*, over miniature bridges, past the shops and restaurants behind St. Mark's and down to the waterfront. Not the Molo here but the Riva degli Schiavoni, where these days it wasn't Slavonic merchantmen that tied up but the No. 5 vaporetto. She turned onto the spacious Riva, glanced enviously at the five-star Danieli Hotel, and nearly bumped into Max Silverman coming out.

It was automatic to say hello and wonder if she'd dropped a brick when he looked embarrassed. A few seconds, then reason took over. The embarrassment wasn't social.

And in the same few seconds it vanished and he was his urbane, sybaritic self, flattering her with his soft voice. She remembered the voice from Brazil; it filled a room like an opera singer's pianissimo. Maxwell Silverman was draped, as always, in roomy, beautifully tailored clothes which he wore with the carelessness of the born rich. He was big and fleshy, though hardly fat. He was growing a dewlap and the eyes had little wrinkled pads all round them.

She could never see any expression in those eyes, and that, with their surrounding cushions, made her think of lizards. Chameleons, perhaps, because the rest of the face was always changing.

"And how long are you here?" she asked.

"Ah. There you have me. It's hard to tell. Business can be so unpredictable. And that, if you won't think me ill-mannered, puts me in mind of my appointment."

"Of course. You mustn't let me keep you."

Then a demon got into her. She looked into his eyes and held out a hand in a way that invited him to kiss it, and he did. She spun it out as long as she could and said, "Dear Max. It's so lovely to see you again," with what she hoped was controlled emotion.

It worked. He clung on to the hand and kissed it again, quite enthusiastically, and by the time he looked at his watch and insisted he really must go, he had collected her phone number and promised to ring when his plans were more settled.

She watched him walk away towards the Molo looking pensive

and slightly flat-footed, and smiled and thought, Middle-aged? There's still some mileage left in the old bag. Let's have some fun.

She had better change her appearance. She stuffed her cloak in her bag. The hat followed, and if it didn't recover, who cared? She was sick of it. She could work in the Cini any time. Today she would follow Max.

She let him go a hundred yards before setting off. She broke into a run when he vanished over the Paglia bridge; she hung back while he passed by the Doges' Palace and the mouth of the Piazzetta and stopped at the Cipriani landing stage. He's going across, she thought. What do I do now? Wait till after lunch? He could be hours. Have a drink, anyway. She sat down outside the café on the corner and ordered a *spremuta d'arancia*.

Fresh orange juice. Healthy, ladylike, expensive. Good for the soul, she thought, fishing in her bag for something to read. Do I really have to do this? Hello, who's that?

The hotel launch had come in and Max hadn't gone on board but was coming back towards her with one of the passengers. A bony, red-haired woman in white slacks, a puce chiffon blouse, and orange sunglasses. Dido panicked. If she'd any sense, she thought afterwards, she'd have slipped inside the café till they were clear. But she didn't, and he saw her. He looked away fast, but she could see the surprise on his face, and the embarrassment again. This time it stayed longer. She concentrated on the depths of her bag, pretending she hadn't noticed him, while he pointed at something across the water and started talking to the red-headed creature.

Go on, said her demon. He's seen you so it doesn't matter. Be a devil! She took off to intercept.

Max, forewarned, looked only mildly surprised. "Hello. What's happened to your hat? I thought you were going the other way. Elsa, my dear, this is Mrs. Marsden. She saw what they did to São Paolo."

She shook a hand covered with rings and asked, "Mrs. Silverman?" A clanger after meeting Carmen, but the devil was in her so serve him right. A man who could pass off that Brazilian jungle cat as his wife was fair game.

Max smiled, except his eyes, and said, "My lawful wedded wife."

You're clever, she thought. You're clever and you're not at all scrupulous. And as for you, poor thing—she looked at Elsa's painted face—you've suffered and you're suffering now. I must be extra kind to you.

"I was so sorry about your place in the Dorsoduro," she said, nominally to Max. "Another one. It's dreadful. Do you think they'll catch them?"

"Who knows? I very much hope so. It's all getting rather tedious, isn't it, my dear?"

"Tedious, he calls it." The wife sounded terribly on edge. "It's downright scary. I mean who's safe? Oh, Max, why do you have to make these enemies?"

Enemies? Smooth, diplomatic Max?

"My dear, I am who I am. These attacks aren't personal, I assure you." He was looking at Dido, not his wife.

"So you keep telling me. But what I want to know, Mrs. Marsden, is why us twice over. I mean, look. We've got London, Paris, New York, Milan, São Paulo, Venice—that's six, and they've gone for two already. That's two attacks out of four—I mean it *has* to be personal . . ."

"Four? I didn't know."

"Four. There's been one in Holland and one in England, and both of them old friends. And in Holland someone got hurt."

Chief Inspector Corti had said nothing about that, and nothing about Mrs. Silverman. But why should he? All he'd wanted her to do was tell Captain Montani he thought he'd seen Max, and help them to keep in touch.

"But I'd no idea. How frightful. And is it . . ."—she hesitated, wondering how to put it tactfully.

"Anti-Jewish?" said Elsa, and she liked her for it. "Yes, it is."

"Who are these people? Does anyone know?"

"Not really. Unless the police . . . You heard about that trouble on the plane?"

"What plane? Oh, wasn't there something about a hijack?" Dido was no great newspaper reader, except for the arts pages, and no great radio listener either, and she hadn't even got a telly. The past was more interesting, and safer.

"Our English friends had chartered it, you see. And the pilot was one of the hijackers. We're hoping the police will have got something out of him—he was a pretty feeble specimen."

"Why? Were you . . . ?"

"Yes, I was there. Oh, don't worry. It was over in twenty minutes."

"Thanks, apparently, to Sir Galahad from Scotland Yard," said Max.

"I'm afraid I didn't pay much attention . . ."

"A man called Corti," said Elsa, and Dido, who sometimes wondered if she was what paranormalists call a "sensitive," felt thundercloud vibrations issuing from Max, or at the very least a passing frown.

"Corti?" she said. Delicate ground? She didn't care. "Corti? But I met him."

"He went for the pilot, you know. It was jolly brave of him—I mean he didn't know the man had a gun, but he must have known he might have."

Max frowned again. "A very parfit gentle knight, no doubt. But this must be rather painful for you, my dear." Not her, Dido thought. Him. "And now if you'll excuse us . . ." His eyes were trying to express something but making a bad job of it. Telling her she was an interfering bitch? Or that if it wasn't for his wife, he'd have offered her lunch? Or both? The vibrations were inconclusive.

"Of course," she said. "So nice to have met you, Mrs. Silverman."

"It's getting a little late, Max," said Elsa. "Oughtn't we to go straight there?"

"If you say so, my dear."

She went back to her *spremuta* and watched them walk back past the Cipriani landing stage and on towards Harry's Bar and the vaporettos. They'll be going across to their gallery, she thought. Shall I follow them? Oh, what's the point.

The next vaporetto at their landing stage was a No. 1, which zigzags up the Grand Canal with stops on alternate banks. Its first was at the Salute, and even at that distance Elsa's white and puce signalled that they were ashore and heading towards the Galleria Silverman.

Dido finished her *spremuta*, ordered some toasted sandwiches by way of an early lunch, and remembered Captain Montani. She'd better ring soon or everything would be shut till four. She went to the phone booth and got Montani's *capo* again. He sounded suspicious and annoyed, and she began to see what the Chief Inspector meant. No more phone calls to the office, she thought, I'll have to do better. Perhaps I could catch him at home this evening.

Meanwhile her *tosti*, the vaporetto to San Giorgio Maggiore, and the art library of the Cini Foundation.

She was home and it was suppertime before she remembered the captain. There were only three Montanis in the directory. She got him first time.

She made herself known and passed on Corti's message about Max, plus her own account of meeting him. The captain thanked her gravely.

"And, *capitano*, he asked me to tell you he is finding difficulty in telephoning you officially. I also . . ." She filled in the details.

"Thank you, Signora. Thank you very much indeed. You will not expect me to say more, but believe me, I am deeply obliged, both to you and to the Chief Inspector."

"He would like you to suggest some way he can reach you in confidence."

"I agree. But the method requires thought. If in certain quarters confidence in me is indeed insufficient . . . We are on the telephone, Signora; it could be unwise to go into detail. But you may be sure that by some means or other I shall communicate with our friend."

"*Capito.* And if I can be of any further service . . ."

"You will be informed. I am grateful that you should offer. And now, Signora, I have taken enough of your valuable time . . ."

The day after that was Saturday. She tried to work, sorting out her notes from her session at the Cini. But her heart wasn't in it. And it was a relief when, in the afternoon, her doorbell rang and an academic-looking character in spectacles and a lot of hair addressed her as *professore*.

"Not professor," she answered. "Just signora."

The character held out a hand and said, "Montani."

Her jaw must have dropped because he laughed. "You must excuse me for behaving like a person in an opera, but it is best to take precautions."

How life imitates art, she thought. Let's hope it doesn't make it a habit. Aloud, she said, "*Capitano!* Come in. Sit down. Can I offer you anything? Coffee? A drink?"

"Nothing to drink, thank you, but last time we spoke you indicated an offer of assistance."

She didn't quite panic. "That's right."

"I am grateful, Signora. And the offer remains open?"

"I think so."

"Then it would be advantageous if I could communicate with the Chief Inspector through you."

"Why not?"

"You could use your telephone to transmit and receive messages, and if there is a need for direct conversation, I could perhaps come here and use it myself."

"I will be honoured, *capitano*, but . . ." International calls weren't cheap.

"The expense? I shall naturally reimburse you. You have my word as an officer."

She smiled. "No problems then."

"Only that of our own communication. It is prudent that it should not be open."

"I suppose not." This was very Venetian and exciting. "What do you suggest?"

"Nothing complicated. I have a friend—well, a person who can be trusted—who has a stall in the Campo Santa Maria Formosa. You can see it from your window. The greengrocer."

"Which one? Oh yes. Mamma Chiara."

"You know her?"

"I shop there sometimes."

"Good. Then if you should wish to communicate with me, you should speak with her. Ask her simply if she has seen Giorgio lately. Alternatively, it will be easy to hand her a note with any small payment you may make. She will get word to me, though you must understand that I move about the city and it may take some hours. If you wish to speak with me, you should indicate it.

And finally our names. In all our communications I shall be Giorgio, you will be Dido, and the Chief Inspector will be Franco. Silverman's name should not appear. Signor Argentino, perhaps. *Va bene?*"

"*Va benissimo.*"

"And now, Signora Dido, perhaps we could inform our friend. You have his number?"

She got through to him at Scotland Yard quite easily. "Mr. Corti? This is Dido Marsden. I've seen Max. He's staying at the Danieli. And someone called Giorgio wants a word . . ."

CHAPTER 10

NO SCREAMING

Sunday was Mass in St. Mark's—she liked going though she wasn't a Catholic or even much of a Christian—followed by idleness and the whole of *The Magic Flute* on records. She lay on a huge Italian settee with her eyes shut and let the music possess her. Like God, if you happen to be a saint, she thought, and nearly as therapeutic.

Monday was routine. A party from the Friends of Grinling Gibbons was due in Venice that evening; on Tuesday she was to introduce them to the city, and thereafter she would be with them for much of the week. She checked their programme. She could handle it in her sleep.

It would be a relief, too, to get away from those policemen. Helping behind the scenes had been fun to begin with, but some of the things Giorgio Montani had said to Corti on the phone had alarmed her. "Assassinio? Murder? Today? I am glad you told me. And the new identity? Please spell. Owen Leppard. Thank you." And later he had repeated other names. "Meyer? Yes, Mossad, definitely. No, I do not know where he is." Then, "Gobboni? Ah yes, the pilot. I regret that I have no access. They say he talks freely but I do not think he knows much. Their security is quite good . . . The boy's father? Manfred? That is noted. No, no other incidents . . . *Ciao*."

Murder! she had thought. And Mossad! Isn't that the Israeli secret service? What have you got mixed up in? You stupid impulsive cow. For a while she was very frightened. But when Max Silverman rang on Monday and invited her to dinner that evening she accepted on the spot.

She spent the day in a state over her clothes. She was glad Mrs.
Silverman was around, or she might have had misgivings. When
she arrived at the Danieli, in a blue and gold kaftan, and Max
greeted her alone, she assumed his wife was merely late.

But after two champagne cocktails—strong ones, because they
felt like twice as many—Max said, "Shall we go up then?"

"Up?"

"We're dining in my suite. I thought it would be nicer on our
own."

"The three of us?"

"Just you and me."

"But your wife? Isn't she . . . ?"

"Sadly, no. My Elsa . . . But this is not the place for
confidences. My voice carries, so they tell me, which is why I prefer to dine privately."

If she'd been fully sober, she would probably have walked out,
but the cocktails had set off her demon. She could look after herself. She laughed. "Well, you cheeky old so-and-so! All right. But
you'd damned well better behave."

Max was shocked. How could she possibly think . . . ? If it
had so much as entered his head that she could take it amiss . . .
Would she rather they ate in the restaurant? It would inhibit his
conversation, but he hoped not to the extent of boring her. A
pity, he implied, but her wish, as his guest, was law.

She sighed. "It's all right, Max. Just play it how you like." Was
that ambiguous? She hoped not, but the drinks made it hard to
tell.

The suite consisted of a small lobby, a large double bedroom
with a view, a small dressing room with none, a palatial bathroom, and an infinity of cupboards. Their table was laid in the
bedroom, with champagne in a silver ice pail and a bowl of roses.
She suppressed a fresh urge to run and said, "More champagne?
Are you *sure* you're going to behave?"

"If you wish it, my dear." So it was only if she wished it now,
and she was damned if she was his dear. But she could hardly
blame him after calling him "dear Max" on the Riva. Besides, she
felt flattered. If a man fresh from that Carmen creature picked on
her, in a city famous for its women, she must be wearing better
than she thought.

And whatever Max Silverman's ethics, there was no denying his charm. He dressed so well; he'd found a modest little pink for his buttonhole and his suit and shirt and tie were conservative with the right dash of cad. And he went in for what some people would call "old-world courtesy." The constant implied flattery, the business with coat and chairs and after-you-my-dear. And his worldly-wise art trade gossip, which was interesting as well as fun. The sort of girl who went in for sugar daddies could do worse.

"Can you eat oysters, my dear? If not, then . . ." She could indeed. Waiters came and went, the champagne was vintage and really beautiful, the food light and delicious. "In Venice one should normally eat fish, don't you think? Unless of course you prefer . . ." She didn't. He had chosen *sole Véronique* and it was perfect. She began to enjoy herself.

"That was lovely," she said, turning to a salad as pretty as a bunch of flowers. "Thank you, Max. Now tell me about yourself. You were starting to say something downstairs."

"Ah, poor Elsa. It's a very sad thing, but she seems to have taken against me. A brave woman and the best wife a man could have wished, and I still adore her, but . . . We never had children, you know. Perhaps that could have soured her . . ."

She was in a credulous mood by now, but not enough to swallow that whole. Not after meeting Carmen, and not after talking to Mr. Corti.

"We're in different hotels, you know. We had to meet; we have business to discuss. That's all of our relationship that's left. Business." The voice registered pain endured with courage.

She listened with genuine sympathy, and he seemed to respond. "I might as well come clean, my dear, if gossip hasn't done it for me. I have, shall we say, legal difficulties which make it imprudent for me to return to England. But London is where our business is based—mine and Elsa's, because much of it is in her name . . . Let me fill your glass."

He had done it before she could stop him; it was the fourth time at least and the bottle was barely half empty. Bottle? Dammit, the thing was a magnum! She must take care.

Max, once started on his own affairs, was in no mood to change the subject. "It's all so sad, Dido." It was the first time he'd called her that. "I slave all my life to build up that business, I hand half the share capital to my wife, I make her a director, though you understand she has never worked there, except now and then to help out. I made it a point of honour that she shouldn't need to work, and she never has. And it was all going so well . . .

"And then this damned policeman has to . . . Yes. Well, least said soonest mended. Suffice it to say that I have never wished any man harm except in protecting my own. But the Italian temperament is not like ours . . ."

"Italian? I thought you were talking about London."

"I was. But it is my misfortune that this good old London bobby happens to come of Italian stock. Florentine, actually; his father used to do cleaning and restoration for me, and *what* a master! He's dead now, poor old man." For a second Max shivered from head to toe. His eyes fell shut and opened with a cold hate in them that was quite frightening.

". . . So his *bloody* son—excuse my language, my dear—his son has to come hounding me as if he is conducting a vendetta. I had to sneak out of my own gallery, in a false beard if you please, and leave the country very fast indeed."

This was getting too good to be true. Her demon, as drunk as she was, woke up. "Do you always keep a false beard handy?"

He emptied his glass, refilled it and went smooth again. "Let's say the need for precautions had already become apparent."

"So you're here to sort it out with your wife. Your English wife."

He looked distant, then said with a suaveness exceptional even in him. "We're splitting it down the middle, and when the operation is complete, our lives, ourselves, and our concerns will be in different hemispheres of the globe."

The waiter brought cheese and dessert, and for a while they reverted to small talk. She was sorry for Max, as for any victim, but that didn't mean she took his side. "Poor Max," she said. "And this policeman—you don't mean . . . ?"

"Yes indeed. You know him, don't you? The airborne Sir Galahad. My enemy, though it grieves me to say so. I hope you and he are not too friendly."

She had enough sense left to say, "Friendly? Good heavens, no. I only met him once."

"How, my dear?"

This was beginning to feel like an interrogation. The voice was unbelievably silky. Dare she tell the truth? She hoped so. She was too fuddled to lie.

"Through the carabinieri. You see, I saw a picture of your gallery door, after . . . And, do you remember, I'd seen the São Paulo damage as well, and those swastika things . . . I mean it *had* to be the same man, didn't it? So I went along and told them. And Corti was interested too—he was here on holiday—so they put us in touch and we had lunch together. He's back in London now, I think." She liked that "I think."

"It was public-spirited to volunteer your information. Let's hope they put it to good use. I suppose that in this particular matter I must regard Sir Galahad as not quite an ally but what I believe is called a cobelligerent. Ah—excuse me a moment."

The telephone by his bed had buzzed discreetly, and Max Silverman, with no sign of haste, had crossed the room and picked it up before he finished speaking. *"Pronto.* Silverman. Ah, Manfred . . ."

It was only a short conversation, and Max spent most of it listening, while she thought, Manfred? I've heard that name before, and very recently. Where? On the phone, when Captain Montani was talking to London. I must tell him about this, and Corti too. I wish I knew what it was all about. I mean what's Max done . . . ?

But Max was saying, "Excellent. Here, then. Thursday," and hanging up and ringing for coffee. "And a glass of brandy, my dear? Or a liqueur, or . . . ?"

She declined and put a hand over her glass against the last of the magnum. The interrogation seemed to be over. She curled up with her toes under her kaftan in an armchair that had been built for crinolines and relaxed while Max looked avuncular and approving and talked in his mellow voice. But when the waiter cleared the table and went, she was not too addled to know it was now or never. She got up to go.

"Max, darling, that was lovely, and terribly sweet of you . . ." She made to kiss his cheek, the way she'd kiss any friend after a good evening and found herself pushed back into her chair.

"Oh, no you don't, my girl. You've got some explaining to do."

She was too stupefied to reply. He stood over her, very big and close. Her eyes were at a lower level than his waist, and her awareness of him was strongly physical—like being confronted by some large male presence in early childhood—and not entirely alarming.

But it was an effort not to shiver. After a moment she said, "Max, dear. Really!"

"I'm glad you say 'really,' because this is very much, as the vulgar would put it 'for real.' The world of men, my dear, has a very crude expression, as well as a strong distaste, for a woman who puts down a man she has enticed. I warn you that I am not easily put down. Furthermore, I flatter myself that, though no longer young, I am able to give a woman considerable pleasure. These hands are very knowledgeable, my dear. And, apropos, may I say how delightful you look when startled? Charming, quite charming."

She ought to have been furious. She *was* furious. But she was flattered, and a very small bit of her could almost have given in. His effrontery! He almost deserved to get away with it.

Meanwhile she was expected to say something. She cast around for words. "You—you old . . ." Strong language was, she felt, in order. "You lecherous old *sod!* How *dare* you speak to me like that?"

"How dare I?" he said. "Dare? Do you think I am endangering myself? *I* should be thinking in terms of danger? Not I, my dear."

"Is that a threat? What on earth are you talking about?"

"You, my dear, and your remarkably equivocal behaviour. You break bread with my enemy. Thereafter we meet, apparently by chance; you make sheep's eyes at me, you spy on my movements, and then set out to annoy me with pointed references to my marital affairs. I can only conclude that you are in league with the police, though remarkably inept about it." His voice had dropped till it was almost a whisper.

"You're drunk," she said.

"And what if I am? You drive me to it. Do you want me to behave like a drunk? Because I'm tempted, by God!" Suddenly he was shouting at her, harsh and high pitched. "What the hell d'you think you're playing at? *Bitch!*"

On the word "bitch" he slapped her face.

For a moment she was numb with shock. Then fear took over, and not the half-enjoyable fear of a few minutes earlier. It cleared her head.

She knew she must get away. She knew she didn't want a scandal. No screams, then. And short of screaming there was little she could do, cringing in her chair with Max standing over her. Unless, if she could get to her handbag . . .

"Dido, my dear; just because I've drunk a little wine, you mustn't make the mistake of thinking that was unconsidered. It was not, and it was not meant lightly. These hands are not only knowledgeable, they are very strong. It would be wise to answer my question. What are you playing at, Dido?"

He was standing between her knees with his own against the front of the chair, and his presence was overpowering. She wondered whether to hit him where he was vulnerable, but he must have been watching her eyes, because he said, "No, my dear. I shouldn't advise violence. It wouldn't work. And I shouldn't make a noise either; it could harm your reputation. Mine doesn't matter, you see; that's gone. If I were you, I should accept the situation."

"What situation? What are you trying to say?"

"That you are here in body and so am I. That you have set out to attract me and succeeded. That I am very much stronger than you, and an accomplished lover. That I desire satisfaction. And that you will not leave this room till you have given it. Oh, Dido, my darling . . ."

Was this how accomplished lovers talked? She was thinking very clearly now. "Oh, Max. Dear Max. I'm afraid I've upset you terribly, but I'm not up to anything sinister, truly. It was just . . . Well, Corti was asking about São Paulo, and he knew I'd met you there. So naturally we talked . . . He was making such a mystery out of everything . . . So when I ran into you . . . It was pure curiosity, Max, and if I behaved badly, it was simple naughtiness. I can't help it; it gets me into awful scrapes sometimes . . . Well—look at me now!"

She laughed. It wasn't difficult, in fact it could have got out of control.

"Dear Max," she said, and held out a hand. "I'm *so* sorry."

He didn't move or speak at first, but when he did it was to take her hand and kiss it. Then he said, "Make it up to me."

She made herself smile up at him. He helped her to her feet, and she said, "Just let me go to the bathroom first. Where's my handbag?"

He handed it to her. She could see him feeling triumphant, in no hurry now, not asking so much as a kiss.

"Shan't be a moment," she said.

In the bathroom she opened the bag and took out a scent spray. She'd carried it for years, though more from habit than conviction now she was no longer a girl. It was an odd place to have to use it. She pointed it away from her and squeezed to make sure it still worked. Even like that the fumes made her eyes smart.

She flushed the loo for the sake of the sound track, and emerged into the lobby. Max was invisible. She slid to the door leading to the corridor and tried the knob.

He had locked it while she was in the bathroom. She went back to him.

He was at his dressing table in his shirt-sleeves, with his back to her, and as she came into the room she saw him put the key with its unmistakable hotel tag in a drawer.

Give him one last chance, she thought. She said, "Max dear. I'm not feeling awfully well. Would it be very terrible for you if I changed my mind? Another time perhaps . . . ?"

He whipped round, very fast, and looked at her. Then he came towards her, slowly and deliberately, rolling up his sleeves.

She drummed up a smile and said, "You win, apparently." She was standing with her hands and the scent spray behind her, half aware but no longer caring that the attitude emphasised the swell of her figure under its kaftan. She moved towards him, swaying a little and hoping she didn't smell of ammonia. "Here you are then, Max, dear. Satisfaction."

CHAPTER 11

CHUMS

She pitched her deep voice for the young man standing at the back. "Ladies and gentlemen, welcome to Venice, and first of all to this rather special part of it, because you are standing on deeply historic, I nearly said holy, ground. The Molo. The doorstep of Europe. On this spot, for a thousand years, travellers from the East . . ."

A mild breeze drifting up the Adriatic stirred her hair. Behind her, the crescent of waterfront stretched away towards the Lido. In front, the graceful bulk of the Salute, pale in the Canaletto light, presided over the Grand Canal. The Friends of Grinling Gibbons stood listening, their heads turning in unison as she pointed out the landmarks.

". . . And to my right, the Piazzetta leads us to the great square, or Piazza, and the Basilica itself, the great golden shrine of St. Mark, which you can see protruding beyond the Doges' Palace, and which, in a few minutes, we shall visit . . ." The heads followed her pointing arm. The feet, not yet wearied, rested unfidgeting on the pavement. Here and there a camera pointed and blinked.

"And now, shall we walk up the Piazzetta? The building on your left . . ."

They were the usual sort, not yet distinct as individuals; a mildly prosperous, mildly cultural mishmash. Most of them were women and middle-aged or older, and of the half dozen men only the one at the back looked interesting. He was younger than the others, and stood a little aloof as if he thought himself a cut above them. Perhaps later she could help to thaw him out. Meanwhile, the Campanile.

She had a headache after last night and was talking on automatic pilot. She had to. She was shaken and frightened, though she wasn't sure what of. She had slept badly in spite of Max's champagne, and had had bad dreams. One had been about swimming in the Canale Orfano and being tried for it. There had been skeletons. Walking that morning to the far end of the Riva degli Schiavoni, where the Friends were staying, she had gone round behind the Danieli. It would be a long time before she passed its front again.

The worst thing was not having talked to anyone. She'd got back too late and disturbed and sozzled to telephone London and had surfaced too late that morning. But she had bought a lemon —it was in her handbag now—and asked Mamma Chiara if she had seen Giorgio, and Mamma Chiara had shaken her head expressionlessly and taken the cash.

She wasn't sure how much to tell Giorgio, but she could talk to Corti, who was understanding but too far away to intervene. Had she overreacted? Would he really have taken her by force? It was hard to believe it. People in the art world, or at his level in it, just didn't behave like that. Nor did they threaten to. Nor did they invite women to their bedrooms and lock them in. And he was drunk, he'd admitted it, and he was under enormous strain. Wanted by Scotland Yard, attacked by Nazis, his marriage and his business falling apart. He'd wanted her, and he'd seen her as a threat.

A cornered rat? She was convinced he'd have done it, or tried to. So in military fashion she'd carried out a preemptive strike, and in nonmilitary fashion felt guilty afterwards. But what was the alternative? Lie back and enjoy it? Not a chance. And nothing less would have worked. She hoped she hadn't damaged his eyes permanently.

Anxiety, guilt, self-justification, round and round like a recording on a loop, were a ground bass to the whole morning. She could feel it even while she spoke.

". . . And that in 1902, when photographic apparatus was heavy, cumbersome, and slow, very early one morning, at a most unsocial hour, a photographer should have just happened to be in the Piazza with his camera all set up, and that at that precise moment the Campanile should have just happened to fall down, must be about the strangest coincidence known to man. If indeed it was a coincidence; but few have suggested otherwise. It is, after all, quite hard to fell a campanile. But the photograph exists and is well known . . ."

So far, the young man had stood about, always at the back and in faintly arrogant poses, looking bored and paying little attention. But he smiled now. He was better looking when he didn't: pale and dark, but with surprisingly light hair, and a mouth which at rest was the classic Cupid's bow. She had a feeling his smile was less at the coincidence than at the falling tower.

She covered its rebuilding and Sansovino's Loggetta. She showed them the restored grand portal of the Doges and moved on to St. Mark's Square and the Basilica.

The trouble about St. Mark's, if you had a hangover, was the floor. It had been subsiding unevenly for a thousand years and was correspondingly squiffy, and the many-coloured inlaid patterns made it worse. She steadied herself against a marble column and started her recitation. It felt as thin as the gabble of the Doges' Palace guides.

The young man had genuflected when he came in, but was looking supercilious again, like a certain sort of artist at an exhibition. You'd see them sometimes, stalking round as if they were God and if you came too close they'd zap you with the lightning. How vulnerable they must feel. She must try to put him at ease.

She got her chance when they were filing round behind the high altar to look at the Pala d'Oro (which started as a Byzantine altarpiece and is pure jewellery and would seat sixteen if you used it as a table top). She found herself beside him.

"Hello," she said. "Is this your first time in Venice?"

He edged in front of her to present his back. Normally she might have let him be, but today wasn't normal. She tapped his shoulder. His jacket felt like plastic. "Excuse me, but are you all right?"

He murmured something without turning his head.

"I'm sorry, I couldn't quite hear you. Is there anything I can do?"

"You can . . . Thank you, I am not in need of your services." Only his head turned, and his expression, like his voice, started not far short of vicious and ended tame but cold.

"I'm sorry, I didn't mean to intrude, just break the ice a little. After all, we *are* in Venice."

This time he looked her in the face. His eyes were strained, she thought, and older than the rest of him. He opened his mouth, shut it again, and turned away.

She gave up trying. Poor dear, she thought, waiting for the rest to gather round. He *is* frightened.

After St. Mark's they broke up to find their own lunches. She went home and stopped at the greengrocery stall, but there was nothing from Giorgio. She rang Scotland Yard. She wondered how to ask for Corti without his surname, and decided she couldn't. But he was out. She left word that Dido would call his home that evening.

The afternoon was a running fight through the Doges' Palace, where the guides ran a closed shop and didn't appreciate scholarship. It was a long trail too, and no shortcuts. By the time they were halfway round she felt quite faint.

They trailed over the Bridge of Sighs to the cells and a lot of claptrap about Casanova. They trailed back, and there on the bridge was a friend. She fell into his arms.

"Nigel! Oh, bless you. How on earth did you get here?"

Sir Nigel Trehoward, P.R.G., R.A., gave her a smacking kiss and laughed. "Hobnobbing with the *direttore*. Pulling rank." The Principal of the Royal Gibbonsian Foundation could do things like that.

"I thought you weren't joining us till tomorrow."

"So did I. But it was pouring with rain in London, a dinner date got cancelled, and I thought of you struggling with the Chums. So here I am."

"Well, bless you again. You don't know *what* I've been through . . ."

He was a dear, a bearded, brown, quick, elusive Celt, who painted abstracts that almost everyone liked, and in under two years as principal and without making enemies, he had galvanised the poor old Gibbonsian more than anyone thought possible. He liked to join the Friends of Grinling Gibbons on their jaunts, especially when it was Venice, and blow their minds with a bit of modern art. She felt better now he was around, and better still when he invited her to dinner and a good cry on his shoulder.

"I'll cry buckets. You'd better bring a towel."

She was within an ace of it there and then, but the uptight young man was passing, with his face turned firmly away, and she pulled herself together.

"Who's that guy?" Nigel Trehoward asked when he was out of earshot. "Any idea?"

"No. I thought he looked lonely and tried to chat him up, but he wouldn't have it."

"Funny. His face seems to ring a bell. Perhaps it will come to me. Look, I mustn't stop now; just came to show the flag. See you this evening."

It got her through the afternoon. Out on the Piazza she left them to their own devices and went home.

But not to peace and a lie-down, because Giorgio, in his academic guise, was on the doorstep. She gave him tea all'inglese, which he sipped very politely, while she passed on the news. The Silvermans in their separate hotels, dividing their empire, the expected visit from someone called Manfred . . .

"Manfred? Are you sure?"

"Quite sure. The name came up when you were talking to Franco, so it caught my attention."

"Have you told him?"

"Not yet. He was out. I'll try again this evening."

Half of her wanted to talk about the Danieli episode, but the other half overruled it. It wasn't she who had got hurt. Besides, it was her word against his, and even British policemen had the reputation of caginess about that sort of thing. So in Italy, with its southern machismo . . . And if they did believe her, they might want to pull Max in, or even prosecute, and then it would be in the papers.

So she kept it to herself. Giorgio thanked her for tea, left it to her to tell Corti about Manfred, and went.

The tea had finished off the hangover, but she couldn't settle to anything. She lay down but couldn't let go; she picked things up and put them down; she tried to meditate but didn't know the technique and got bored; she couldn't think of a book she wanted to read. She was glad when it was seven and Corti should be back at home.

He was. And it was still raining in London. And, though he said little, there was a sense of anger, almost of menace, in his voice. It's partly the timing, she thought; the little pause while he takes it in and decides what he's not going to say. Suddenly she was pouring her heart out about last night's dinner.

This evening's with Nigel was better. They ate at her favourite, very local *trattoria* in a dark alley a yard wide, where tourists came only through accident or expert knowledge. She was known there, and Nigel, having made the owner laugh with his bad Italian and paid outrageous compliments to his wife, was judged *simpatico*, which led to things like drinks on the house and unscheduled goodies in the cooking. It was a good evening.

She told the story of her and Max for the second time, and she did cry, but less than she expected, and Nigel was marvellous. She talked openly about the police, and when she mentioned the Scotland Yard Italian he said, "But I remember him. He got us back our tondo." The Gibbonsian tondo was Michelangelo's secular counterpart to his equally famous one at the Royal Academy. "What's his name? Frank? No, Franco. Franco what?"

"Franco Corti."

"That's the chap. Tough cookie. Knee-high to a dachshund and looks like a Roman emperor. We made him an honorary Chum. Which reminds me," he went on with his mouth full, "that guy with the Chums. I asked Janet." Janet, secretary to the Friends, was shepherd, dogsbody, and fixer to the tour. "Name of Leppard. And I remember who he reminds me of: a lad we had as a student. A sculptor. I didn't care for his work. Didn't much care for him, as a matter of fact. Have some grapes."

She nibbled them absently, thinking, Leppard? and wondering whether the lock of brown hair that flopped over Nigel's left eye was maddening or attractive.

"It was thinking of Corti put me in mind of him. The tondo caper. The boy was with us at the time. In fact, rumour had it he was mixed up in it, but I never heard officially. It was before I was principal."

"Oh? And what was the gentleman's name?"

"Springer. Leo Springer. He was darker than this lad, but apart from that they could be twins."

But this one was called Leppard. She'd heard that name too. First Manfred, then Leppard. Owen Leppard. She'd heard them at the same time, when Giorgio was talking to London. "And the new identity?" he had said. "Please spell."

"Leppard?" she said to Nigel. "His first name wouldn't be Owen?"

"I think it is. How on earth did you . . . ?"

She told him.

"Oh," he said. "Oh. So he's got a new identity. And what, I ask myself, was the old one? And the police are taking an interest . . ."

"And there were rumours about the boy who looked like him? Twins, you thought? Brothers?"

"Why brothers? Why not the same? A bit of dye on his hair . . . Why not? Dido, I'm beginning to think the Chums are harbouring a viper in their bosoms."

"Oh, no! This is too much. First it's helping a pair of nice policemen, and rather fun. Then it's Max turning horrid, then this Manfred, whoever he is, and now this. Great black crows, Nigel, flapping round my head. Like Jung, poor man. It happened to one of his patients. They haunted her. They used to mob her. Real live crows; he saw them himself. It's the most terrible story . . . They think it's related to poltergeists."

"Rooks, I expect," he said. "I like rooks. Crows are solitary and much nastier. Cheer up, ducks. Look, let's ring Franco and report. It's only half-past ten in London."

It was only a short walk to the Campo Santa Maria Formosa, but she was glad he was with her. The narrow *calli* of the quarter had turned sinister, but no one attacked them, and the square was deserted. "Up here," she said as they stepped out of the moon shadow.

Three arches sprang from the *campo* over the little canal called the Rio di Santa Maria Formosa and carried steps up and then down to three front doors. She loved the approach to her flat; in moonlight it was piercingly beautiful. She wanted to cry again.

Inside, Nigel refused coffee. He had been right, and Corti hadn't gone to bed. She told him about Owen Leppard and meeting Nigel Trehoward and Nigel thinking he recognised him. "Do you want to speak to Sir Nigel?"

He did.

"I'm right," Nigel said when they had finished. "It is young Springer. We're asked not to make him suspicious. Do you think you can cope?"

"I'll have to, won't I?"

"You could get flu. Leave the Chums to me and Janet."

"No, no. I'll be all right."

She was less frightened now she was at home. She said good-night without a twinge. "And thank you for a lovely evening."

"It was fun. See you tomorrow."

She wrote a note for Giorgio before going to bed. There seemed no point in asking for a meeting. In the morning, having slept better than she dared hope and feeling very secret-agent-ish and hardly frightened at all, she slipped Mamma Chiara the note with the money for a couple of persimmons. Then she walked, avoiding the Danieli, to the Friends' hotel at the far end of the Riva. This morning Janet was with them. She helped her herd them onto the vaporetto, then from the Grand Canal to the Gothic barn of a church known as the Frari and behind it the Scuola di San Rocco, with its vast hall painted all over—walls and ceiling—by Tintoretto.

The buildings weren't her favourites, but she liked the quarter. She took them through the Frari at a smart trot, dwelling only on its Titian. She expounded the San Rocco Tintorettos till she was sure she had bored them stiff, and after answering their questions went to pay her respects to the Christ in the corner. He was life-sized, made of wood, and very old and primitive, and the art historians mostly ignored him. But his eyes stabbed like lasers, with a force that made Tintoretto and the rest look like posturing decorators. Why did she love their city so much? . . .

She turned away and met eyes nearly as fierce, which eased as Leo Springer brought them under control. She could think of nothing to say. Nor could he. The smile he produced reminded her of wolf-whistling youngsters on the street. She thought of police records and violent crime and the Canale Orfano.

What did a man like that do? Work? Batten on women? Steal? Nigel had said he was a sculptor, but that wasn't a living unless you were Henry Moore or someone, or unless you taught. Did he teach? A man like that? Never.

And what did he do in Venice, in the evenings or the long Italian lunch breaks? Her demon, quiescent since the evening with Max, had a suggestion: find out.

So, when he left the Scuola di San Rocco, she followed. He headed south, then east, following the curve of the Grand Canal a block or two away. Behind the Accademia, on the threshold of the Dorsoduro quarter he rang a doorbell and was let in.

She kept walking and noted the address. At home, she typed it out for Giorgio and caught Mamma Chiara knocking off for lunch. They had the *campo* to themselves and could talk. The earlier note had not been collected yet, and as a friend of the *capitano*, perhaps the Signora would accept a bunch of grapes as a gift.

What lovely people, she thought, and went back home. She was finished for the day now. She ate most of the grapes for lunch and went to sleep.

The doorbell woke her, and Giorgio in long hair and glasses greeted her smiling. "Signora! I have come to express my gratitude. The information you have given me today is of the first importance and the greatest value to me personally."

"Is it?" She was only half awake. "I'm so glad."

He was in a forthcoming mood and she got an explanation. The house near the Accademia belonged to a carabinieri major called Caccia. "I think it is because of him that communications about these people have not reached me. I could prove nothing, you understand. But now that a known terrorist . . ."

"Terrorist!" She had difficulty controlling her voice. "Terrorist? My God! . . ."

"It would perhaps be wise if you did not try to investigate him further, now that I know where he is."

"I should think it would! Can't you arrest him?"

A smile. "That could be premature. He has influential friends. But of one thing I can assure you, he will not leave Italy. Indeed, he may not easily leave Venice. When does your tour end?"

"Monday." This was Wednesday.

"Let us hope he remains with it till then. *Coraggio*, Signora. He has no cause to harm you or any of your group."

She hoped he was right. There were four whole days of him ahead.

Meanwhile Corti had to be informed. They caught him at the Yard and Giorgio spoke to him. He put the phone down looking amused.

"Signor Leppard has enemies, Signora. It seems there has been a fire."

CHAPTER 12

ROY OF SUNSHINE

That was on Wednesday, and in London quite a lot had happened since Saturday and Charlie Little's death. The case belonged to the Surrey force and Pierscombe to North Wessex, but the London ends of both were Corti's.

And that meant Charlie's brother, the safe breaker Roy. Corti hadn't called him to the Yard but phoned and promised to stick to Charlie's murder, and Roy had positively invited him to his home. So at eleven on Monday morning he had walked there in pouring rain fom St. John's Wood tube.

The house skulked, ugly and red and twenties, behind a high brick wall topped with spikes. He pressed an imposing bell push by the garden door and announced himself over the intercom.

"Gate's open now, guv. Leave it open, will you? It shuts automatically."

The dark path, between high, clipped, soaking laurels so close together he couldn't help brushing against them, reminded him of that dead-end Venetian *calle* the night Elsa Silverman lost her way. It ended on a dank band of crazy paving, with beyond it a front door painted black. There was a second intercom here which reproduced Roy's voice so well he thought for a moment he was speaking through the letter box, only that was on the street door.

"Come in, guv. Second door on the right." The tones were dull and chesty, with no attempt to talk posh.

It was like walking into a miniature science museum. The hall was full of glass cases containing models of every kind of machinery. Some were working. A closed-circuit TV camera watched him from above.

The second door on the right led to a large room with south-facing French windows starved of light by a wall of conifers. The room smelt as if the windows were seldom opened. Roy Little, silhouetted against one of them, came forward to shake his hand. "Morning, guv. I'm glad as it's you. Well, they had to send someone, didn't they? I was afraid it might be that Billings again."

"Roy?" Keith had said. "Proper little Roy of sunshine!" No one else had laughed. Poor sod, Corti thought, villain or no villain; they were that close. Roy and Charlie had more in common than you might think.

"Roy," he said. "I'm sorry. All right, he was a thief, but I reckoned him. Both of you."

"He was a good brother and a bloody good screwsman. Kept us both out of trouble, didn't he? Dunno how I'll get on without him . . ."

This was not the blank gloom he had met in the past, but penetrable, as if for once Roy was glad of someone to talk to. Corti took in the walls of technical books and science fiction, the closed-circuit TV, the Daniel Quare clock, the astrolabe or orrery or whatever, the nondescript, almost shoddy, furniture; Roy Little in a zip-up cardigan with a big floppy collar, looking prematurely old.

"Here, guv. It's nasty out. Have a scotch." He thought he'd better accept.

Roy's scotch was Glenlivet. He poured about an inch and a half into public-bar tumblers, aligning the two surfaces carefully. His own glass had been used already. Roy had never been seen the worse for wear but was known to run on the stuff. There was no water or soda in sight.

Corti prepared to do his duty. "To his memory then." The whisky stung like fire but tasted glorious. "Ninety proof?"

"Hundred. If we was in America it'd be a hundred and fourteen point two. It's the only stuff's worth having."

After a second sip Corti was inclined to agree. "Well," he said, when they had settled down. "D'you want to tell me?"

"Dunno who done it, if that's what you mean."

"Likely then? You knew I'd been to see him, did you?"

Roy nodded lugubriously. "Went to put a few bob on at Ascot, didn't we? Hour or two before it happened. He done quite well, did Charlie: must've won a couple of grand."

"Any luck yourself?"

"Me? You're joking. Lost a sodding monkey, didn't I? Five hundred quid. Know what, guv? What's the use, I sometimes wonder. I mean there he was, poor sod. Flash wheels, flash bird, flash gaff. Anything he wanted. And was he happy? Nah. That Mandy led him no end of a dance, his kids were no pleasure to him, and as for young Wayne . . . Made his life a bloody misery, didn't they, what with one thing and another."

"Thought he was scared of young Wayne."

"Sodding right he was scared of him. Kick your teeth in as soon as look at you, would that git. Do his old man over, do anyone over. Bleeding skinheads . . ." Roy looked round for something to spit into, didn't find it and muttered to himself instead.

"Skinheads?"

"Hell's Angels. Whole frigging mob of them on these dirty great bikes. It was Mandy as gave him his, stupid cow. Conned poor Charlie as she wanted the money for some tom." Tomfoolery equals jewellery.

"You never married, did you?" Corti said.

"What'd I want with that? Kids as'd only grow up villains? Nothing but a load of trouble, the whole frigging business. Don't get me wrong, guv. I like my bit of unders, same as the next man, and I'm willing to pay for it. But no strings, guv. I don't want no bleeding strings. My gaff's nice and handy for Lord's, I got my hobbies, got a man and his wife to look after me, a woman as comes in to clean. Got my freedom, ain't I? And when you think of poor old Charlie . . . Sorry, guv."

Corti waited till he had recovered. "You were telling me about young Wayne. Got form already, hasn't he?"

"Nah. Only speeding. Managed to keep his licence, more's the pity."

"How old is he now? Eighteen, nineteen?"

"Nineteen next month."

"Still no job?"

"You've got to be joking."

"Could he have done it, Roy? His own father?"

"Jesus, guv, I wish I knew. Yes. He could of. Got a temper, hasn't he? Goes raving berserk. I never seen nuffink like it. I remember once, his dad and me was watching the test match on the box—couldn't hear a thing because of his bleeding stereo. So

Charlie asks him, nice and reasonable, could he turn it down a bit. Know what that boy done, guv? He just screamed and picked up that telly and put it through the winder. Quarter plate glass and all. You never saw such a mess. We had to get Mandy's portable . . . Yus. I reckon if young Wayne had his blood up, been boozing or mainlining or something . . . He could've done it, guv. Not in cold blood, mind; that ain't his nature, but if he was crossed . . ."

The Surrey CID would be asking the same questions, but mightn't be getting the same answers. Not from Mandy. From her daughters? She had two. They must be twelve or fourteen years old, but apart from that they were unknown quantities. He couldn't even remember their names.

Roy poured himself another Glenlivet.

"And if it wasn't him," Corti asked. "What then?"

"You tell me, guv."

"Leppard," he said, "Owen Leppard. Does that mean anything to you?"

Roy's face went blank.

"It's all right, Roy. I'm not at the con. It's still Charlie I'm on about. It was him as named that name, see, and the very next day he got done. This Leppard's got form abroad. He's a paid-up terrorist. A killer, Roy. So think about it."

Roy put his hands over his face and started to tremble. Corti ought to be trembling himself. "Stand on me, Charlie," he had said. "I'll look after you."

Meanwhile Roy was going to cough. Any minute now, he thought. Poor little sod. After a while Roy blew his nose and started swearing with such concentrated venom that Corti was quite glad when he stopped.

"Leppard, Roy. What d'you know about him?"

"Off the record, guv? Got a deal, have we? Yuh. He was with us when we done Pierscombe and if you're the man I think you are, I never said we done nuffink. And if you're not, you can put me away tomorrow and I wouldn't give a monkey's."

Corti nodded sympathetically. "You've got your deal, Roy."

"Bloody foreign bastard."

"*Why*, for God's sake? Why him?"

"He had information, didn't he? He was going to shop us,

wasn't he, if we didn't do like he said. And what he says is, keep right on screwing, but stick to the Children of sodding Israel what deals in antiques and that, and His Lordship's coming along to see as we does it right. *Him* seeing as *we* does it right!

"So, seeing as we ain't made our minds up how to get shot of him, and we been thinking about Pierscombe since Block first had it, we give it a try. The homework was mostly done. So it sort of fell into place, didn't it?"

"And Chummy came too?"

"Yuh. And a sodding awful time he give us. Takes all the pleasure out of it, having to work with a berk like that." Corti made sympathetic noises. "And I'll tell you another thing: you know how he left that gaff? All messed up, and his flaming Nazi signs and that? Well, if it hadn't have been for me and Charlie, it'd have been a lot worse. Got a really filthy mind, that boy has. You can have him, guv. He can shop me and good luck to him, 'cause I don't give a bleeding toss."

Corti's last sight or sound of Leppard or Springer or whatever he called himself had been the voice on the radio of the Rent-awing Cheyenne. If that was whose it was. And that was how long ago? Not quite a week.

"We was at Lord's, see, watching the Pakis, and this geezer comes up and blows down Charlie's ear. Know what he says, guv? He fingers four houses what was our last four jobs, and then he says, 'I think we might cooperate, don't you?' So we has to take it from there."

"How did he know?"

Roy shook his head. "That's what we asks ourselves. Dunno, guv; he wasn't letting on. You need time to get to the bottom of things like that."

"Could it have been him?"

"Why not? If that's true what you been telling me about him. Stands to reason, dunnit?"

"What for, then?"

"Dunno. Could've got it into his head as Charlie'd snouted on him. Well, he had done, hadn't he, if it was him what give you his name."

"Yes, but Leppard wasn't there. No one was there, only me and Charlie."

"Didn't have to hear, did he? He'd only got to know as you'd been there . . ."

"Tailing him? Hiding in the bushes?"

"Nah. Could've been Mandy, though. Couple of gins and Mandy'd tell him anything. Been making up to her, hadn't he, right under Charlie's nose, and sort of leering at Charlie while he done it. Shouldn't be surprised if they was having it off, guv, and if Charlie hadn't of been the easygoing sort . . ."

"It couldn't have been that, could it? A punch-up over Mandy?"

"Not worth the hassle. That's what Charlie used to say. That Leppard wasn't the first, you know. And Charlie wasn't no bleeding monk neither."

Corti nodded. "What they call an open marriage, eh?"

"Marriage? Get away."

"Two kids and fifteen years? What's the difference?"

"Fair enough. Here, have a drop more scotch . . ."

Towards one o'clock they both started looking at the time. Corti had his date with Bruce Zappaterra.

"And I got someone coming here." Roy looked knowing, and Corti understood why when, on the pavement outside, Roy's visitor flashed him a grin. She was black and very young and wore tight scarlet knickerbockers. He wondered what she cost and how much she was allowed to keep.

The Trattoria was barely half full when he reached it, five minutes late, and strode through under the plastic vines to the private alcove, where Hector Dando, smooth-faced and spruce in his white dinner jacket, went into his maître d'hôtel routine for him. His English was pretty good by now. "Welcome, Chief Inspector. Madame Teresa asks me to say she is busy in the kitchen. I trust you are well after the accidents of your holiday?"

"Great, thanks. Mr. Zappaterra not here yet?"

"Not yet, Chief Inspector. What can I bring you to drink?"

"Nothing, thanks. I'm up to there with scotch."

Hector looked desolate behind his spectacles but Corti was wise to that. In the early days he would have changed his mind out of sheer kindness.

"A soft drink, then, Chief Inspector? Tomato juice?" He capitulated.

So it was with tomato juice in hand that he greeted Bruce Zappaterra. Bruce's colour of the day was blue, even his shoes. The man himself was scraggy and brownish-grey with matching hair, a matching, nicotine-stained moustache, and large brown eloquently pleading eyes. Little Tony had christened him "Mr. Zapp" and zapped everyone with invisible-ray guns when he was mentioned.

"Ah, Franco. Good morning. I'm sure you won't mind: I've brought John Bennett to join us." The lawyer was behind him. How like him to bring someone when you were paying.

But Bennett had good news. He was nothing to look at but had earned Corti's respect in court many years earlier. "The valuations are agreed, and there is every prospect that the picture will be accepted. If you wouldn't mind signing . . ."

Bruce's righteousness, now that Bennett had blessed his papers, was quite touching.

"So that's it then?" Corti said when they had signed.

Bennett smiled. "We should get probate quite soon now, and . . . I think I can safely say it's over bar shouting. Congratulations, both of you. You're quite a rich man, Franco, and fortunate in your coexecutor. I shudder to think how we would have managed without Bruce. Your father chose well."

"So no more tax to come out of the residue?" he asked after due acknowledgement. The residue was his children's.

"No. The potential trust fund stood on Friday at one hundred eighty-nine thousand, seven hundred seven pounds."

"And my own bit? Not Butter Court—just the pictures. After tax of course."

"I expect probate for approximately a third of a million."

He'd known it was on the cards but it was still amazing. His Italian blood, laced with Glenlivet, took charge and before he knew what he was doing he had kissed Bennett on both cheeks. And then Zappaterra, through an aura of cigarettes and yesterday's Aramis.

"Hector," he called. "Champagne! The Krug seventy-three. A magnum!"

CHAPTER 13

FIRE

He rang Bennett from the Yard. "Those things you said about Bruce, John, were you just being nice to him?"

He wasn't. Bruce was really a remarkable fellow. His persuasiveness, his grasp, his mental agility, his knowledge of the Inland Revenue . . . He'd worked like a slave, he couldn't hand in his bill like a qualified accountant . . .

"I can't say I trusted him a lot." He was full of drink and he'd known Bennett a long time or he wouldn't have said that.

"I'm talking about his ability, Franco. Ability and loyalty. To those, it may be inferred, who are loyal to him."

"Meaning I ought to see him right? How much?"

"In your shoes, I would think in terms of a thousand to fifteen hundred, and I would be inclined to regard it as an investment."

This was amazing. Perhaps he'd underestimated Bruce. He took the plunge and asked what he'd never dared. "John—you're sure it's not a fiddle?"

"I don't see why it should be. Nothing's been held back. He's presented the facts in the most favourable light, naturally. That's what we're there for."

He heard his father's voice: "It is yours, Franco. I give it to you. A chattel of two thousand pounds. There will be no tax, nothing to declare, eh? . . ." Bruce hadn't wanted to know about that, and Corti had never quite got around to telling Bennett.

And now apparently the picture would go, as part of the old man's business assets, in lieu of capital transfer tax. And Bennett said no fiddle. He remembered Elsa Silverman on Italian attitudes to taxation. Suddenly he felt self-righteous. Who was he to tell Bennett it was a fiddle when Bennett said it wasn't? And if that was thinking like his father, why not?

The picture was a little *Annunciation* and associated with Fra Angelico. The experts agreed it was from his workshop but not about how much was from his own hand, and its provenance, which had once looked doubtful, had turned out to be right. He hated the thought of losing it.

But the National Gallery had thought it worth having, and they seemed to want to hang it, so he'd be able to go and see it.

"Franco? Are you there?" He'd almost forgotten Bennett.

"Sorry. Just taking it in."

"Don't forget Bruce, will you?"

"I won't. Thanks for telling me. See you, John." He got out his cheque-book wrote Bruce a cheque for fifteen hundred pounds, remembered his bank balance, and tore it up.

He groaned and searched his desk for an Alka-Seltzer.

Head still swimming, he tackled the heap of paper. He countersigned two urgent reports on cases coming up next day without reading a word. He thumbed through a list of goods stolen in Hamburg without seeing it. Concentrate, damn you, he told himself, and back came the refrain. A third of a million! And Butter Court, and no tax! Franco Corti, you're rich. So why in the name of all the saints are you sitting in a poky office shuffling bits of paper?

But the next one was a copy of his four-day-old all-stations message, and clipped to it were two replies.

Both told him about thefts from dealers, signed with holed swastikas over Stars of David. Both lots of loot were thought to have gone abroad. As at Pierscombe, the things stolen were small but valuable. Weintraub of Augustine Antiques in Canterbury specialised in snuffboxes, or had till they were all taken; Stein in Birmingham was a High Street jeweller but also a well-known horologist and had lost all his antique watches. Corti remembered seeing the list not long before his holiday, and for all he knew he'd seen Weintraub's as well. It would have gone out internationally. But the Canterbury job had been six weeks ago, not many days after Pierscombe.

But the style was different. Weintraub was still in hospital, and at Stein's the thieves had hidden in empty premises over the shop and come through the office ceiling as soon as the staff had left. In the middle of the rush hour, with the alarm ringing merrily and no one taking a blind bit of notice.

Springer or no Springer, those jobs were never the Littles. The West Midlands law weren't doing well over suspects—the job didn't fit any of their villains—and the best Kent could come up with was "a London gang."

He rang the two CIDs and asked for the full score, including photographs of the graffiti. He made sure the lists of stolen goods had been circulated, to Interpol as well as nationally, and that there had been no response. Then a thought surfaced, dislodged perhaps by the mix of Glenlivet and champagne.

Venice. Lists of stolen goods. The Galleria Silverman. The Pierscombe list had gone out like the others and should have found its way to the dealers who mattered, including Silverman International. And however crooked Silverman was, he would be mad to stock bent gear openly in a place like Venice. But that was what he had done.

Or what his manager had done. Was he really that stupid? Surely not. So either he had some ulterior motive or he didn't know the goods were bent. Carelessness? The list not reaching him? Italian bureaucracy could be slow, but a whole month?

Ulterior motives then? Unlikely. If he knew the things were stolen he could end up inside, and he wouldn't want that. Unless of course there was collusion, and in Italy, once you got into that territory, anything could happen. All the same, it could be worth finding out if Gasparin had seen that list. The more he thought about it, the more he suspected he hadn't, but with his head in its present state thinking hurt and wasn't reliable. He picked up the next case docket. It was as much as he could do to read.

He knocked off at 5:30 sharp for once and trailed home through a clammy drizzle, dreaming of the Grand Canal in the autumn sun, of seafood and wine on its banks while gondolas slid under the Ponte di Rialto, of Teresa in their bedroom at the *pensione*, pouncing. He grunted. She'd better not pounce tonight. Come on, boy; get a move on. Get some fumes out of your system.

Turning into the cul-de-sac that was Butter Court, he persuaded himself he was better. It was a dingy backwater of small craftsmen—specialists, repairers, outworkers—and too out of the way for the sex barons or he'd never have come there. Its sole public attraction was a struggling Bangladeshi restaurant. Half Soho had been like Butter Court once, but not any more.

The house that had been his father's studio, gallery, and living hutch was at the end. He had hated taking down the sign by the front door, with its handsome, grimy lettering that for thirty-five years had spelt out, ANTONIO CORTI, PICTURES RESTAURED, GALLERY. But now, with a coat of paint, windows that actually opened, and pot herbs in window boxes, you had to admit it was more welcoming. He could go in now without a shudder. Perhaps it was the children or perhaps the alterations, because the office where his father had died had been split between two other rooms, but the ghost was laid. Things had to be bad before the place upset him.

Teresa would be at her Trattoria, but the children would be home. Corti's slit mouth lengthened and lifted a full eighth of an inch. He felt almost happy as he tapped his "Dad's home" rhythm on the lounge window.

Gino stepped into the little hall at the same moment as he did. He closed the lounge door quietly and whispered, "Hi, Dad. He's here."

"Who's here?"

"The Wally."

"Eh?"

"Wali Mohammed. Sylvie's Paki."

It was all he needed. He danced a boxer's feint and jab towards the lounge, and wished he hadn't. "*Madonna!* What's he like?"

"Oh, all right. Gets a bit stroppy about race and that. Can't blame him really. His brother got duffed up by greasers. And he doesn't reckon the Old Bill either; doesn't like their manners. He's been stopped more than once. Red rag to a bull, actually. It was a job to get him to come here."

In the fullness of time the Joint Sub-Committee on the Community Policing of Ethnic Areas would secrete its pearls. For swine, no doubt; meanwhile the poor pigs were on their tod. And Franco Corti, with a head like a pressure cooker and a mouth like a hyena, had to do his bit for race relations, peace, and his darling

Sylvie. At least he supposed he had. He took off his wet mac and hat, squared up, and made his entry.

Wali Mohammed stood with solemn politeness to shake hands. His was small-boned like a girl's.

"Hello, Wali. Is that right? Wali?"

"Yes, sir. Pleased to meet you, sir. It's very good of you to invite me to your home." So he'd invited him, had he? It was nice to know. There was nothing Eastern in the way the boy talked, unless it was a certain gentleness.

"Well," said Corti. "Don't stand on ceremony, sit down. What would you like—tea, coffee, Coke . . . ?" Tea was strictly for when there were visitors.

"No, thank you, sir."

Silence. The boy must be scared out of his mind, and so must Sylvie. The younger ones were into their best behaviour act and Corti was all tensed up and afraid of showing his feelings. It was Gino who rescued them.

"Tell Dad about Pakistan, Wali."

"All I know is what my parents say. Their village was in the Murree hills, very nearly in Kashmir. There were pine forests. I think it was very beautiful, sir."

"You needn't call me sir, you know. You're not in the job yet."

"In the job, sir?"

"A copper. A racist pig, eh?" He could have bitten his tongue off.

Wali Mohammed froze, and Sylvie burst out, "Oh, Dad!"

"I'm sorry, pussycat. No offence, Wali. I didn't mean . . ."

"No one does, do they, sir?" said Wali. "Bye, Sylvie; been nice knowing you."

"Wali—no!"

But Wali had gone, followed by Gino, and Sylvie was crying and shouting, "Pig! Pig! Pig!" and first among the cauldron of guilts inside Corti was the one about being a policeman.

But Gino brought Wali back and it was smoothed over. Rocco from the Trattoria brought food that Sylvie only had to warm through. Wali told Corti about his grandparents' white draught cattle and terraced fields by the Jhelum River, and Corti told Wali about his own grandparents' vineyard at Panzano-in-

Chianti, which belonged to Uncle Paolo now, and where he
thought there were white draught cattle too.

But Wali wouldn't touch wine, even watered, and soon, before
Teresa got home, he left, and Corti dragged himself to bed.

He was fit; he was forty years and six months old. He woke up
feeling good, with Teresa asleep beside him. His routines went
normally and at half-past eight, sweating from his walk to work,
he sat down at his desk.

The Birmingham and Canterbury details came by first des-
patch. He started with the photos. The holed swastikas looked
like the same man's work but were crude and lopsided compared
with the others.

All that the documents told him was that both jobs were professional and done by teams of three using stolen vehicles. The
descriptions from Canterbury were sketchy and conflicting. The
stolen goods lists added nothing. Special Branch had been informed, but without result. He scribbled a memo for Towler and
put the papers out for filing.

The morning ground on. He hated desk work, and the higher
you climbed the more there was. Some time after eleven a telex
appeared.

Reference your 28 Oct all-stations circular . . . On investigating suspected arson 13 Camden Terrace, NW1, landlady
states lodger answering description K.L.O. Springer left yesterday 1 November. Star of David graffiti found on garden
wall . . .

He grabbed a pool car and took off.

Camden Terrace was parked cars and small low Victorian
houses with token front gardens. No. 13 was a gap in the roof
line, a devastated garden, and charred holes for windows. Two
small Asian children and half a dozen assorted adults stood about
staring. The fire brigade had gone, but there was a policeman in
uniform at the gate and a forensic team inside. Corti made himself known.

Two hours later he sat down to a plate of lukewarm spaghetti
in a Cypriot restaurant and mulled over what he had learned.

One, it was Springer all right. He had used the name Owen Leppard and the landlady judged him creepy.

Two, he had settled up and left at six the previous evening, and the fire had started nine hours later.

Three, subject to full forensic reports, it had been started under his bed, probably by one of the more horrific chemical mixes, with a crude timer incorporating an alarm clock, a torch battery, and a clothes-peg.

Four, the Star of David by the front gate was yellow, and the holed swastika which it partly obliterated was not obvious on the grimy brick.

And five, the handwriting of the graffiti was new to him.

Which added up to what?

Superficially, to an attempt by militant Jewry to burn Leo Springer in his bed. Alternatively, to an attempt by Springer to make it look like that. Nothing else seemed to fit. If Manfred Block hadn't given his word that the law would be respected, he would have inclined to the more obvious explanation.

So if it wasn't Block & Co., then what about Springer? It was in character, as far as he could tell. But certain things didn't fit. The graffiti weren't like his, and Corti doubted if he would think of disguising his handwriting. And the firework? An amateur job, surely. Clothes-pegs, from an activist of the Vaterländerbrüder-schaft? He shrugged and called for his bill.

In the car there were other things to ponder. Bruce Zappaterra and a third of a million's worth of pictures, and his salary that would be topping up his bank balance about now. And Gino. How well he'd handled that situation, and he was only fifteen.

But as for poor Sylvie . . . they'd always been so close, like with all his children. And suddenly this crevasse had to open. He didn't kid himself Gino had closed it. What had Teresa said, and it had seemed so ridiculous at the time? "Turning them into little revolutionaries . . ."

Crossing the park to the Yard, he thought of his father and their long estrangement. Twenty years, and all because he'd chosen to join the law. The law his father had lived by was that of family. Twenty years, and all right, in year twenty-one they were reconciled. And in year twenty-two the old man was dead. Corti growled aloud.

And now his lovely Sylvie, screaming "Pig!" like some hellcat at a demo. Was it really that wicked to serve the law? His emotions said it was. He tried to be firm with them, but they didn't give in till he was at his desk writing another memo to update Towler. It couldn't be that wicked to discourage people from burning each other's houses.

The evening was wet again. Not long after he got home, Dido came through, thankful to have found him at last and badly upset by a passage of arms with Maxwell Silverman which made him so angry he found it hard to sound as sympathetic as he was. Her real news was that Silverman was expecting someone called Manfred on Thursday. He grunted his thanks, made a note to tell Towler in the morning, and returned to his domestic worries. Angst all round, Sylvie refusing to speak to him, her mother taking both sides at once.

He went to bed early, but his first sleep was broken by the telephone. Dido again, plus Nigel, telling him Springer was in Venice. Must have gone straight from Camden Terrace to the airport. He didn't have much of a night after that, and the one time he was properly asleep must have been when Teresa came to bed, so he missed his chance to talk about Sylvie.

Next morning at the Yard there was a fresh reply to his circular. It had come in from Interpol, Paris, by telex, and reported a three-month-old theft of ivory carvings in Vienna. A violent one again. Jewish dealer, holed swastika; the mixture as before. The news, plus Dido's from the night before, joined the flow of paper. Another memo for Towler.

He stayed chairborne till late afternoon, when Giorgio came through yet again. They've gone telephone mad, he thought, but changed his mind when he heard about Major Caccia. It was nice of Giorgio to pass on things like that. He reciprocated with the Camden Terrace fire, and as soon as they had finished he rang Towler.

"More news from my Venice contacts, guv. Springer's there, alias Owen Leppard. Slipped across on a cultural package, cheeky sod. We know where he's staying, and he's been seen calling at a carabinieri major's home. Name of Caccia. Probably the one who's shielding him."

"Oh yes. You said something in one of your memos. I don't

know what's come over the carabinieri. They used to be bloody
good, you know. We had a hell of a job to penetrate them in the
war, in fact I'm not sure we did. I'd like to think it's just the odd
rotten apple."

"So would I."

"Never mind. You're bringing in information. Is that your Captain Montani?"

"Partly. Plus luck. Plus my civilian snout."

"D'you want to give me a name?"

"Not a lot, guv, if you don't mind."

"Hmph. So Venice is where it's at. Block's booked out tomorrow, that's confirmed. A booking for two, the other one's Victor
Aaronson. That ring a bell?"

"Not offhand. Which hotel?"

"The Danieli. Same as your friend Silverman."

"Will your lot be keeping an eye on them?"

"Do you think we should?"

The policeman in him saw the point. Block was a law-abiding
citizen, and what he did abroad was his affair. But every nerve in
him was shouting, Silverman! He's going to see Silverman!

"Well, guv . . ." He hunted for the right words. "He didn't
deny it, did he, when I put it to him he was masterminding a
war."

"All right then. You do it. No need to fly, just see 'em on
board. My lads will see you right to the plane. Then get your
carabinieri chum onto the other end."

"Right, guv." He hung up, jotted down the flight details, told
the switchboard to ring Venice, and called in Detective Sergeant
Billings.

"Keith. You know Manfred Block by sight. He's leaving
Heathrow tomorrow, 1330 hours, flight BA522, with a bloke
called Victor Aaronson. Get onto Photographic and go with
them. Contact the airport SB. They'll be expecting you. Picture
and full description of Aaronson, right?"

"Okeydoke, guv. Will do."

A minute later he was through to Dido, but Giorgio had left.
"Damn. How soon can you get a message to him?"

"I could ring him at home, but I don't think I ought to, do

you? I think he's afraid his telephone's tapped. Otherwise I don't know. Some time tomorrow?"

"Damn," he said again. "All right; don't risk it. But get this to him as quick as you can: Manfred Block's flying to Venice tomorrow with a man called Aaronson. Flight number BA522. Will he keep an eye on them please?"

There was nothing else he could do. That name Caccia was really weird. Italian for "hunt." One for Dido's collection of coincidences. He spun out his paper work till after six and went home to an evening as bad as the last, except that he did get a word with Teresa.

"But I thought you knew," she said. "Someone at the school's feeding them propaganda. She'd never heard of politics before, and what does she get now? We're racists, we're establishment lackeys, we're oppressors. Specially you. The police are a plot against the workers . . ."

"*Madonna!* Is it really that bad?"

"It will be if you don't do something."

He didn't sleep well that night.

Next day some more came in about the Vienna ivories. Some of them had been recovered. He sat up and exclaimed, "*Mamma mia!*"

They had been recovered in Venice, and a dealer called Abrami had been arrested there for handling stolen goods, but released after satisfying the magistrate that he had bought them in good faith. The carabinieri had failed to get their list of stolen art to him.

Must remember to check if Gasparin had seen the Pierscombe list.

And after lunch Keith Billings, hotfoot from Heathrow and Photographic, plonked some ten-by-eight prints on his desk. "There you are, guv. Brother Aaronson."

Victor Aaronson was Shimon Meyer.

CHAPTER 14

FEAR

Block. So that's the mysterious Manfred's other name. How Freudian, she thought, and sat down to type her note for Giorgio. Well, that's one call I won't have to pay for. One to London on Saturday, two yesterday, one ten minutes ago. That's four for my bill already. And Giorgio's a dear, but if he forgets . . . Money's such a tricky subject.

. . . with a Signor Aaronson, arriving Venice flight BA522 tomorrow Thursday. They will stay at the same hotel as *il signor* Argentino. Franco asks you to observe them as a matter of urgency. Dido.

She could see Mamma Chiara, still there, through the window. She looked in the kitchen. She didn't need anything really; perhaps some garlic. She took the note, went out, and stocked up.

She was getting used to this traffic, though it didn't quite seem real. It was normal to pop across in the next morning on the way to the Molo and ask if Mamma Chiara had heard from Giorgio.

"*Mi dispiace, signora, ma . . .*" she was sorry, but of course she hadn't; it was far too early. Well, that was it till evening; it was the Friends' day for the Lagoon.

They were waiting for her on the Molo, where Janet had walked them. Their faces told her she was late again. *Must* get that watch seen to. Not that it would make any difference; she was death to watches. "Am I late?" she said brightly. "I'm *so* sorry. I think my watch must have stopped. Are we all here?"

Janet smiled patiently. "All except Mr. Leppard. He's with friends of his own today."

Thank heaven for that. Dido cleared her throat and began.

"Good morning, everybody. Today we travel north to visit the islands of the Lagoon. We have our own boat, but because of the state of the tide we cannot use the canals this morning but must round the eastern point of the city. We shall pass quite close to the Lido, then spend the morning on Murano, where you will see glass being made and visit the remarkable glassware museum. We shall lunch on Burano and go on to Torcello for the afternoon. Nothing else, Janet? Then all aboard."

The channel by the Lido was a focus for shipping, mainly small craft: working boats, outboard dinghies, sailing yachts enjoying the breeze. The air had a freshness and the light an edge that were missing in the city. It made Venice seem stale, a mere archive, and her life there wasted. She was too young to spend it like that, chewing over dead bones.

To the left the trim rectangles of San Michele floated, laden with tombs and cypresses. As phoney as Venice itself. More so, because unless your family owned a plot, and few families did, they put you in a marble drawer, and twelve years later they took you out onto the Lagoon and dumped you on an obscure island whose name she couldn't remember. Bones on land, bones in the Canale Orfano. In Venice the macabre was never far away.

A long sweep of *briccole* marked the channel to Murano, spread out low and workaday a mile ahead. Warehouses, wharves, a stickle of campaniles. A lighthouse. Soon they were in the canal by the glass museum and stepping ashore.

There was the usual wait while Mr. Johnstone-with-a-*t*-please took photos. There was always at least one pain in the neck among the Chums, and on this tour it was the Johnstones. A pair of squabbling, pernickety old moaners whose yardstick for Venice and everything else was Hove. She wished they'd stay there.

She moved off before Mr. Johnstone had finished. And if he complains, she thought, I'll jolly well complain back and see what happens.

Two hours later they were back on the Lagoon with Burano three miles ahead. Most of the Chums were forward in the little saloon or in the open cockpit astern, but a few were on the miniature bridge with her and the boatman.

She loved this trip. The tiny deserted islands with names like poems. San Giacomo in Paluo. San Francesco del Deserto, away to the right, where friars still walked among the cypresses. The tuft of trees a stone's throw away, with its little ruined chapel, was Madonna del Monte. Why were small things so evocative?

Nostalgia was acceptable again. Her self-questioning mood had gone. The breeze had dropped and only bow waves and ripples disturbed the Lagoon. The air was soaked in light. The *briccole* articulated the wide pale water. On the horizon, Torcello raised a stark finger to the enormous sky.

Then Mr. Johnstone had to come up from the saloon with an impressive telephoto lens on his camera. He looked so pleased with it she wanted to stroke it and say "Good old Freud." He nodded to her, said, "Do you mind?" and edged her out of her place. Next time he did that she would put him in the water.

She looked firmly ahead, where a speedboat was coming towards them, making a lot of noise and spray and shaping to pass close. Ill-mannered brute, she thought. Mr. Johnstone had his camera on it and clicked it just as she recognised the man at the wheel.

It was Springer alias Leppard, and beside him stood an older man she didn't know. He had one of the hardest faces she had ever seen.

A flick of spray, a bump and roll from the bow waves, and the boat was past and heading towards Venice, and Mr. Johnstone was nagging about the splashes on his lens and asking who to complain to.

"You could try the carabinieri. I can't think it would do much good."

". . . Most dangerous, most irresponsible. If no one informs the authorities nothing will be done. My film will be evidence. They will have no excuse for inaction, none at all. You're in charge, Mrs. Marsden. It's your duty to lay a complaint . . ."

The best thing with people like that was silence. If you were polite, they took it as agreement and tried to hold you to it; if you demurred it meant a hassle. She muttered something noncommittal, and Mr. Johnstone shut up and stalked below.

The speedboat had turned and was following them, with no attempt to catch up, about half a mile away. It was out of sight when they tied up at Burano. She helped Janet shepherd the Chums towards their lunch. Mr. Johnstone, thank God, was walking ahead with his wife, camera at the ready and armed by now with a plain non-Freudian lens.

But the Johnstones didn't matter. What mattered was Leo Springer. She was frightened. And puzzled, because why should he turn and follow? Her instinct was to tell the carabinieri—there must be some on the island. But the carabinieri weren't safe, with poor Giorgio having to go through all that pantomime to talk to Franco.

Why? she asked herself. He recognised us, obviously, but why follow? We're no threat to him, for heaven's sake. Unless—my God! Could he have found out? About Giorgio and me and the phone calls? He couldn't be after me? She fumbled in her bag to make sure of the scent spray. It was there and replenished, but gave small comfort. Fine against soggy old Max, but with people like this, terrorists . . .

"Sorry, Janet," she said. "I seem to be feeling a little faint . . ." She had to sit on the ground for a minute or two, with everyone fussing and producing drinks and menthol pads saved from the flight out, and Mrs. Johnstone being an officious bore. She shut her eyes and tried not to listen. If only they'd go away . . .

"Hello, ducks. What's the trouble?"

She opened her eyes. "Nigel! Oh, God bless you! Help me up; I'm fine. Just a touch of the vapours . . ."

"Dear Nigel," she said, arm in arm with him. "You do turn up at the right moments."

"I was coming to join you for lunch, actually. Didn't fancy the glassware again, but . . ."

She told him all about it. ". . . And he's a terrorist! Giorgio said so. A real live terrorist! He could knife us all in our beds, or take us hostage, or . . . Or anything! Nigel, I'm very, very afraid."

He took her seriously, which was nice of him. "Safety in numbers, I think, don't you? It's probably nothing to do with you at all. You'll feel better with some lunch inside you."

But she couldn't eat. She let him bring her a Campari, then a glass of wine, a nibble of salad, and a dozen grapes. She let him bring her a glass of Aurum and take her purse and sort out her

lunch money with Janet. And just as she was beginning to feel
better, all hell broke loose. Mr. Johnstone had lost his camera.

And with it his self-control. ". . . It was hanging on the bloody
chair! *Here!* Am I expected to eat with it round my neck? Am I?
No doubt in this bloody country I am. I shall hold the Royal
Gibbonsian Foundation personally responsible. Where's that silly
bitch Janet? . . ."

"My God!" she whispered to Nigel. "Leppard! Springer! It
must have been. Him or his friend. That man took a photo of
them. They must have seen him and . . . Oh, Nigel! He'll bring
in the carabinieri and spoil everything, and they won't want to
know, and . . . Oh God, I'm going to cry."

"Good idea. Why don't you disappear quietly and get it off
your chest. Leave this oaf to me. What's his name, by the way?"

"Johnstone. With a *t*."

"Right. And Dido darling . . ."

"Yes?"

"It wasn't you they were after, was it?"

As she fled she heard him say loudly in front of them all, "Mr.
Johnstone with a *t*, will you please shut up? I am Sir Nigel
Trehoward and principal of this organisation, and if you want to
throw a tantrum, I'm your man. But not here; you're upsetting
the ladies. Now then . . ."

Afternoon mellowed to evening. They straggled beside the little
leafy canal towards their launch, under trees that shaded their
eyes. It was as pastoral and green as the Cherwell behind
Magdalen. The air was still and neither warm nor cool, but she
would need her cloak in the boat.

The quay was a frontier. The Lagoon, out here towards its
northern end, was largely marsh. There must be nearly as much
land as water. From the quay you looked across a few yards of
channel onto flats that could have fringed the North Sea. A stripe
of land on an infinity of milky light, a calm soft brilliance in
which sky and water were one and the sun, though low and dazzling, was almost lost.

It was an enchanted moment. Part of the magic of Torcello
was this emergence from trees and fields, always late in the day,
always against the sun, into emptiness and light.

" 'The waste of wild sea moor,' " Nigel said as they cast off.

"Ruskin?"

"Right. My second name's Ruskin. Did you know?"

"No. Should I have?"

They laughed. Not even Mr. Johnstone, snapping away beside them, could spoil it.

He was subdued but on the whole happy. His camera had been found in the *toilette* hanging from a peg. Everyone assumed he had left it there himself, and his wife had given him the stick. But he swore he hadn't, and next time he wound the film, there wasn't any. The camera was empty.

But he had been so relieved at having it, he almost forgot to complain. Nearly all the lost film was unexposed, the two or three frames that were exposed were unimportant and he had plenty more in his gadget bag. The whole thing was soon forgotten.

Except by Dido and Nigel. "You know," she said to him when Mr. Johnstone was below, hunting for a filter, "it's a shame, losing that picture. It could have meant a lot to Giorgio."

"Isn't that why they nicked it? I wonder who that other guy was."

"I thought he looked horrid. As if he'd machine-gun you as soon as look at you."

"Big shot?"

"Could be."

"Hm."

"Nigel, I'm still frightened. I'm just not cut out for this."

Before he could answer, Mr. Johnstone was back on deck.

The sun was on the horizon, red now and streaked across with cloud. Sky and water were one big sunset. The *briccole* were silhouettes wearing orange stars. San Giacomo in Paluo, abeam, was pure romance. Nigel's arm settled, welcome and protective, round her shoulders.

She walked home from the Molo through the last twilight, thinking partly about Nigel, partly about Giorgio and how soon she could tell him about the speedboat and Mr. Johnstone's film. Mamma Chiara would have gone home; she must wait till morning. She hoped he'd got her note about Manfred Block and Mr. Aaronson in good time.

The alleys approaching the Campo Santa Maria Formosa were claustrophobic. She had to tell herself not to be silly as she crossed the little bridge behind San Marco into the first of them. She wished Nigel was there to protect her. But you can't have him, she said to herself. He's a married man and he's got other things to think about. I wonder what he's like to live with. Hell, I expect, like most creative people. What a shame. Well, at least it's a change from archives.

Nobody sprang out or grasped her throat from behind. But in the bay on the *campo* between the church and her flat someone was waiting.

"Signora," said Mamma Chiara. "Forgive me for speaking to you like this, but it is important. I am troubled about Giorgio. He does not come; he does not send word, and no one can find him. I could not give him your note . . ."

She summoned all her British sangfroid. "How very kind of you to wait. I expect there's some perfectly reasonable explanation, don't you? But I'm so glad you've told me."

She climbed her stairs, dizzy with fright, knocked back an Italian brandy, and caught Corti at the Yard. "Franco! Am I glad to hear your voice! Look, all sorts of things are happening. Giorgio's vanished; I've seen what's-his-name—Springer—in a boat and there was another man with him and someone photographed them and they stole the film, and . . ."

He took her through the story, patiently, point by point. He was sure there was a perfectly reasonable explanation of Giorgio's absence . . .

He was doing the same job on her that she had tried to do on Mamma Chiara. She must have been quite incoherent.

"So what more can I do?" she asked him. "I mean, if Giorgio isn't around . . ."

"You could do one thing; you could see if you can tell what Block's up to. And that Aaronson. His real name's Meyer, by the way. At least I think it is. Shimon Meyer. I've no right to ask you, mind . . ."

"But how? I've got a tour on my hands. And I wouldn't know how to go about it. Don't you have to be trained?"

"It does help. No, it isn't on, is it? Besides, that Meyer . . . I shouldn't have said anything. Actually, there is one more thing. Abrami, antique dealer, in the Merceria. Do you know him?"

"I know the shop."

"It's all part of the same carry-on. He bought some ivories that turned out to be stolen. If you could find out where he got them . . ."

That sounded manageable. She said, "All right. I'll try," and cursed herself for a fool.

She longed to talk to Nigel, but was afraid to cling. She agonised for half an hour, picked up the phone, put it down again, had another brandy, picked it up and put it down a second time . . .

It rang.

"I'm worried about you," he said. "What are you doing this evening?"

She closed her eyes and relaxed all over. "Cooking spaghetti. Want some?"

After supper they sat a little self-consciously by candlelight, finishing the bottle he had brought and listening to Beethoven.

"Feeling braver?" he asked when it ended.

"I think so. It helps when there's someone around." She was still awash with music.

"Not safe on your own?"

"Well . . . No, I suppose. Oh, Nigel, I know it's not rational. I expect I'm safe as houses, but . . . I imagine things, I get feelings and they won't go away. I work myself into such a state . . ."

"What you want, ducks, is a bodyguard."

"A policeman on the door of the bedchamber?"

"Doors are uncomfortable. What's wrong with this sofa?"

"Nigel! I couldn't! It wouldn't be proper. I mean think, if it got out. Poor Anna."

"Good Lord," he said quietly. "Haven't I ever said? That's what comes of living abroad. No Anna, I'm afraid. Not any more."

"No Anna? But . . ."

"Cancer. I'll tell you about it one day, but not now."

"But how tragic! How long ago?"

"A year last September. So that's settled. You're not fit to be left alone. The sofa?"

"Of course. That is, if you'd rather. Otherwise . . ." Her voice became very small and she felt herself blushing. ". . . Otherwise I've got an awfully comfy bed."

CHAPTER 15

ALL'ITALIANA

Giorgio, Corti thought. He'll be back. He'd better be; that woman's not safe on her own. Ought to stop using her; it's not fair. She's really upset. Glad Sir Nigel's with her; I don't think he'd scare easily.

The family had gone upstairs except for Gino. He offered him a grappa.

"No thanks, Dad. I'm off to bed."

"Before you go, any news of Sylvie's boyfriend?" It was two days since Wali Mohammed, and Sylvie still wouldn't speak to him.

"The Wally? I don't think anything's changed. Except he won't come here in a hurry."

"Be nice to her, Gino."

"If she'll let me. But she's like Mum. Clamps up and you can't get near her."

He had never yet penetrated that mood in either of them. He nodded and raised his glass. "Women. God bless them, I suppose. Thanks, Gino. Good night."

"'Night, Dad."

Women, he thought. I bet Dido doesn't act up like that. Tears, yes. Tantrums, yes, but never silence. This Venice caper's all very well. What if Giorgio's really out of it? Can't use Dido. Can't use Interpol. And Max sits there laughing. Should I go for extradition? Waste of time. It'd take weeks. He'll be gone before it comes through.

What, then? It looks like *all'italiana*. Hector? Bruce? I might have to.

Bennett's assessment of Bruce Zappaterra was sinking in. He must be quite an operator. Furthermore, he must have relations in the Veneto. He must be able to get information, and Hector Dando certainly could, though not especially in Venice. Keep those two on ice, he thought. Call it contingency planning. Giorgio will be back tomorrow, like as not. Come on, bed, or you'll fall asleep in your chair.

"DCI Corti? Mr. Little to speak to you, sir."

"Which Mr. Little?" That was a stupid thing to say. It could only be Roy.

"That you, guv? Listen, I been thinking about poor old Charlie."

He waited. So did Roy. "Yes?" he said at last.

"Yuh. Well. Look, it's all right to talk, is it?"

"Why not?"

"Yuh. Well. You know how it is."

"Come on, Roy. You know you can talk to me."

"It's just—you know—the blower and that."

"A meet then? Is that it?"

"Nah. Wouldn't want anyone to see us, would I? Look what happened to poor Charlie."

"Then the phone's safer. Where are you? At home?"

"Nah. Dunno who could be on the tinkle, do I?"

"You'll be all right where you are. Come on, Roy; we've got a deal, remember?"

"Yuh. Well. Like I said, I been thinking."

"Right."

"And what I been thinking's this. Him what done poor Charlie done him for just that. Knew as you'd been to see him, didn't he?"

"Could be." He'd thought that from the beginning. So had the Surrey law, if they had any sense.

"Sussed you, didn't they, and I been thinking how. Know what I reckon, guv?"

He waited again. "Come on, Roy. Let's have it."

"When you was there, was that boy in the house?"

"What boy? Wayne? He must have been. Charlie thought he was out."

"You seen him?"

"No. But I heard him. Well, his stereo."

"D'you reckon he seen you?"

"He could have. Or he could have seen my car."

"Law car, was it?"

"Right."

"Suss it a mile off, wouldn't he? So what about this? Young Wayne *was* out. But he comes home, see, and there's these wheels outside what he doesn't reckon. So what does he do? He comes in, nice and quiet, and listens. Hears you talking, doesn't he? 'Ullo, he says to hisself, that's filth—sorry, guv; no offence—and in his book that's the worst thing a man can do, talking to f— to the Old Bill. Bleeding paranoiac about coppers, he is."

"Keep talking, Roy." He'd wondered about Wayne as well, though not the detail. That was Surrey's job.

"So that's it, innit? His dreams is shattered, 'cos his Dad's snouting. Never did get on, mind, but he did have some respect. Ain't got none now, has he? So next day he starts in on poor old Charlie, and he's pissed or something and Charlie tells him to sod off and he goes berserk. And that's it."

"You could be right. Mind you, the forensic evidence . . . It's not my case, Roy, but I'll see your ideas get to the right quarter. Thanks."

"He was my brother, guv."

"And young Wayne. Any sight or sound of him, since . . . ?"

"Nah. But that don't mean a thing. I ain't seen him for months."

"And Mandy. Anything?"

"Lot of moaning and groaning, that's all. Poor bitch."

"Nothing else then? Thanks for the bell. See you."

He put a call through to Surrey, couldn't get the right man, and got on with his post. There was a new telex from Interpol. Another swastika job, in Lisbon, with the Portuguese equivalent of GBH but nothing actually stolen. And further down the heap there was another telex. Geneva. Same pattern, but miniatures or small portable objects stolen; Stars of David, holed swastikas; lists circulated internationally—he thought he remembered them from the summer. There was nothing about any property being recovered. He sent messages to Paris asking for photos of swastikas and for details of any recoveries. They'd have them there if there were any and should have circulated them, but these things weren't foolproof.

The next paper on the heap was headed CLARIFICATION. It was about the export of works of art and ten pages long, and he had to read the first sentence three times before he could make head or tail of it.

His brain stalled. It wouldn't let go of those Littles, Charlie, Roy, Wayne. He tried Surrey again and got his man. Murder rated a chief superintendent; this one's name was Fletton. Corti gave him Roy's scenario.

"Right. I'll put it to the lad when he comes round. If he's got any brains left."

"Comes round, sir?"

"Crashed his bike."

He'd done it on the night of the Camden Terrace fire, at one in the morning, on the westbound carriageway of the M3 between London and Farnesford, and his blood-alcohol had been horrific.

His father had been stabbed expertly from behind, upwards under the ribs, with a blade like a stiletto. They hadn't recovered it. It had happened not more than an hour before Corti found him. There was most of three thousand pounds in Charlie's pockets and no sign of a struggle. It looked as if he had been walking peaceably in front of the killer from the house into the conservatory.

Mandy and the girls had been at a school half-term concert and Wayne had an alibi too, though it was only Hell's Angels.

"No, sir, with respect. Not him. Not now as I know how it was done. Charlie had been to the races, hadn't he? He'd have known and looked for the money. And wrong temperament, wrong weapon. His style would be more a broken bottle."

"I agree, or we'd have pulled him and he'd still be in one piece. But he's a suspect and the best we've got. Don't forget his stereo was on."

As if he could. Meanwhile Fletton was waiting for the boy to surface.

He could have to wait a long time, Corti thought, and rang Bill Towler. Towler was more interested in the fire and took the line that if Aaronson equals Meyer, therefore Aaronson fired Camden Terrace, QED. He'd thought about that himself, but the job was too amateurish and also he had Manfred Block's word. Nothing illegal in England.

All the same, he passed the thought on to Holloway, who were handling the job. He told them about Meyer and tried out the theory that the amateurishness was faked. They didn't like it any more than he did, but promised to check.

He thanked them and went back to his "Clarification." It was something he had got to read. It simpered up at him as if it knew it. He growled, stuffed it in his pocket to tackle in the evening, and went out.

He had been back from Venice a week and crime hadn't stood still. He had calls to make at Sotheby's, at a framemaker in Shoreditch, a container depot in Poplar, and a police station in Greenwich. He got back to Charing Cross at half past six, and went straight home.

It was Bonfire Night and the children were heaven knows where. Teresa was at Beak Street. She had left a note: "*Ring Dido. Urgent. PS, Dido?*" *Madonna!* he thought. She thinks it's personal. He dialled the Campo Santa Maria Formosa.

"Franco! Thank God. He's gone; he really has."

"Who? Giorgio?"

"He rang up from Catanzaro."

"Catanzaro? Where's that? Somewhere in the South, isn't it?"

"Calabria. Right down in the toe. He's been transferred."

He swore inwardly and said, "That's a nuisance. Well, I suppose we've got to live with it. Anyway, it lets you off the hook. Plus one or two villains, but that's the way it goes. Well, thank you very much, you've been a real help."

"Oh, but I've got some more for you. We went to see Abrami. You wanted to know where he got those ivories."

"Oh yes?"

"It was a dealer in Milan."

"Did you get the name?"

"Bullo."

"Was it, by God! Now that's really valuable." It was Bullo who had sold the Pierscombe things to Silverman's.

"And you asked me about those two men, Block and Aaronson."

"I did, but I changed my mind. That's no job for an amateur. Specially a lady."

"Oh, it's all right. I haven't been near them. But Nigel popped into the Danieli before lunch. They were there. Max stood him a drink, actually. They know each other."

"You're sure it was them?"

"Manfred Block and Vic Aaronson. He introduced them."

"No idea what they were talking about? No, how could you?"

"I'm afraid not."

"Look, you must stop this. I mean it. That Aaronson . . ."

"Mossad?"

"Dido! You're not meant to know things like that!"

"Giorgio mentioned them to you on the phone."

"That guy's muscle, Dido. You know what that means?"

"Violence."

"Right. So promise you'll keep away. Drop it, or it's me as won't be sleeping."

"You won't get me within a mile of him. Wild horses wouldn't."

"And don't you change your mind."

"I'll be good, Franco. Good night."

It set him thinking about the Lagoon. It was twice that Springer had popped up in a speedboat. Coincidence? On present form, he wasn't likely to find out. The carabinieri were a dead loss now. Well, that's it, he thought. *All'italiana.* Zappaterra. He invited him to dine at the Trattoria Vaccarino that evening and rang in to book.

Hector Dando was dutifully ecstatic. Yes, he would warn Madame Teresa, and perhaps the kitchen would fix a Venetian specialty for his guest. And the wine? Paolo Corti, Riserva 1970? Certainly, Chief Inspector; if he opened it now it should be just right. Two bottles, naturally . . . Only one? Ah—Soave! Perfection!

Not bad for a spy, Corti thought. That reminded him.

"Hector—if I came in half an hour early, could we have a word?"

Lesser men would have told him he was joking—eight on a Fri-

day evening for the anchor man of a restaurant! But Hector was
at his service, body and soul.

Corti changed into his best suit. It was almost black, and bear-
able though inevitably tight-shouldered. He spent a long time
choosing a tie and settled finally for the yellow and white. Like
most of his repertoire it was silk and came from Cousin Matteo's
shop by the Ponte Vecchio. It was broad and striped in the fashion of the seventies, and the yellow was very clear and pale. A
clean white shirt, a careful breast-pocket handkerchief and he
thought he could stand up to Bruce.

Sylvie had kissed him good-night with the others, which was a
good sign. Perhaps tomorrow they'd be speaking again.

"Good evening, Chief Inspector. You will take a Punt e Mes with
me?"

"That's nice of you, Hector. Thanks."

There was something boyish about the pleasure Hector took in
his job. He must be rather a good spy if he could keep up the in-
nocence. It was hard to think of him as an ex-copper.

"Cheers, Chief Inspector."

"Cheers. Listen, I'm in need of a little research. In Milan, actually . . ."

Kid stuff, Hector's smile implied. It was very nearly patronising.

"It's a police matter, but there's a political element and I'm
getting obstruction. The same lot as gave you aggro, I shouldn't
wonder!" The aggro had included three broken ribs and a transfer
to Sardinia. Hector had asked for political asylum.

His face hardened. "At disposition, Chief Inspector."

"Bullo. Art and antiques dealer. Milan. You remember the
Brotherhood of Fatherlands?"

"I remember."

"They're going for Jewish dealers. Stealing. Vandalising. Violence. It's international. Gear from two of their robberies has
passed through Bullo's hands. He's sold some of it to two other
Jewish dealers, and they've got into trouble. The carabinieri are
meant to be investigating, but who knows . . . ?"

Hector was nodding rhythmically and his eyes had a glittering
look behind their specs. "Bullo. That is noted. If you could kindly

give me such particulars as are necessary . . . Thank you. You should have informations within a week."

"And I've got another for you—that is, if you want to take it on. The carabinieri in Venice. There's right-wingers in there and my contact's been transferred away. I daren't go through official channels. It would help if I knew of an officer I could trust."

This time Hector looked serious. He would do what he could but it could take a little longer. What Corti liked about Hector was that he didn't ask questions unless he had to.

"That's great, Hector. Thanks. Where's Signora Teresa? In the kitchen?"

She was. He went down and put his head round the door. She pulled the pan she was stirring to one side and came over to him.

"All right, love?" he asked. Her white toque and apron were spotless. He liked her in them.

She nodded and kissed him.

"Eh?"

"It's all right, Franco. It won't be poisoned. Just give her my love."

"Give who your love?"

"Dido, of course."

It took him a moment to grasp that she was joking. Teresa joking! And about another woman? Before Venice it would have been like Sylvie over Wali Mohammed.

"You remember Dido Marsden in Venice. Her real name's Mata Hari. She's keeping me posted about Silverman's. Actually it's Mr. Zapp."

"Hector told me. I'm inventing you a *scampi Carlina-Vaccarino.*"

"You're a darling." He kissed her again.

"*Buon appetito.*"

His clothes had indeed rivalled Bruce's. The only difference was the tie. Bruce's was tweed and all white.

They laughed at each other—laughter came more easily since Venice—and sat down to antipasto and Soave.

"You were a client of my father's," he said when they were well stuck in. "You've never talked to me about that. Do you collect pictures or what?"

The answer, like most things about Bruce, was equivocal, but his knowledge of the market was not. He was an amateur painter himself, and his cousin had an antique shop in Padua, only about forty miles from Venice.

"Would he know the Venetian dealers?"

"Why not? He was born in Mestre. He goes to the same auctions. Sometimes he will sell to them himself. He will certainly know them."

Perfect, he thought. Leave it for now. He topped up the wineglasses.

"And what about the probate, Bruce?" Teresa had brought the scampi herself, which was unheard of, and they'd been a compensation for those he'd had to leave at the Hotel Cipriani. The Soave was finished, the scent of fine Chianti rose from their glasses; slabs of *bistecca alla fiorentina* covered their plates. Corti stifled the little voice that was whinging about digestion and tucked in.

"It is quite definite," said Bruce. "You pay nothing. The Fra Angelico is accepted."

"It hurts. God, it hurts. But it's for the best. I mean, having to keep it in the bank . . . Here, have some more wine . . ."

After the cheese he gave Bruce an IOU for fifteen hundred pounds. "Services rendered. Sorry it can't be cash; not yet. Once we've got probate I can sell something."

"That may not be necessary," said Bruce. "When we have probate, I shall explain. But for now . . ." He came round the table and embraced him. There were tears in his eyes. His socks were white, for heaven's sake, and the aftershave was fresh. "Franco! You are a good friend indeed! If ever I can be of assistance . . ."

"Well, there is just one little thing," he said when they were back in their chairs. "Venice. Art and antique dealers. Jews . . ."

The Trattoria was nine-tenths empty; the Chianti bottle had been dead for an hour. Bruce had left, topped up with grappa and smoking, at Corti's insistence, a six-inch Monte Cristo, having promised to find out if any more Venetian Jews had been in trouble for handling valuables they didn't know were stolen.

Teresa came up the kitchen stairs in her street clothes and took his arm. Later, asleep in her arms, he dreamt of palm-fringed lagoons full of sharks and speedboats and a telephone ringing.

It was Sir Nigel Trehoward in Venice. It was just midnight.

CHAPTER 16

MUSCLE

Dido, asleep in Sir Nigel's arms the night before, hadn't dreamt at all. There had been no need.

They had been woken by Giorgio's call from Catanzaro. He had been brief and in a hurry to hang up. She had wanted to ring Corti straight away but she was late for the Chums. It was their last day; the Ghetto and the Madonna dell'Orto in the morning, the airport in the afternoon.

"And you'll be with them," she said, putting on her poncho. "Well, darling, it was lovely while it lasted. What a *nice* man you are." Aidan had been clumsy, hurried, and apologetic. She smoothed Nigel's brown swatch of hair clear of his eyes, but it only fell back.

"With them?" he said. "You take too much for granted, Mrs. Marsden. You're not getting rid of me that easily."

"Nigel! You mean you . . . ?"

"How often does something like this turn up? Once in a lifetime? Twice? Three times if you're lucky. I'm not throwing this away, my heart. I'm stopping right here."

"Oh, Nigel . . . Oh! Now you've made me cry . . ."

"And it wasn't just last night either," he said, hurrying hand in hand with her down the Ruga Giuffa.

"But your work! Dinners; speeches; committees?"

"I've briefed Janet. She'll find someone. There's nothing important for a week or two. After that we'll see."

There was no sign of Leppard among the Chums, and the Johnstones were mercifully subdued. On the vaporetto they buttonholed her.

"Mrs. Marsden, there's something Norman wishes to tell you. Come on, Norman. Speak up."

"We have a theory about the theft of my film, Mrs. Marsden. Do you remember the speedboat that splashed us?"

She remembered all right.

"I photographed that boat. There were two men in it, and my good lady informs me they turned and followed us, though I didn't see them. She thinks—we think—they were criminals."

"Go on."

"My good lady has persuaded me it was they who took my film, thinking their picture was on it. They will have seen my lens—telephoto, you see, and quite distinctive—and realised that they could have been—*had* been—shot in close-up. So, as they did not wish their presence to be recorded . . . You take my meaning?"

She could hardly say she'd known all along and was scared out of her wits. "My goodness, Mr. Johnstone, do you really think so? What a *pity* they stole your picture."

"That's the point, Mrs. Marsden. They didn't. It was the last frame on the film. The one that got stolen was a fresh one."

"You mean you've *got* it?"

"I have. And being a public-spirited man I intend, when it is processed, to make it available to the police. We wondered if you knew where we should send it."

"As it happens, I do. I should take it to Scotland Yard. Ask for Chief Inspector Corti in the Art and Antiques Squad. He'll know who to pass it on to."

The Johnstones gawped.

She thought fast. "There was a question of a forgery, you see— a picture I knew rather well. The carabinieri asked my opinion. There was some talk of London criminals being involved, so the Chief Inspector came over and I met him. Scotland Yard's so much safer than the post, don't you think? And no customs forms, no uncertainty, no delays?"

Mr. Johnstone agreed. It was the first time she'd known him agree with anyone. And it was the first time she'd known herself lie like that. She was amazed at her glibness.

It deserted her in front of the Madonna dell'Orto; her account was all muddled till Nigel took himself out of sight and gave her a chance. It was a long, trailing morning. The weather was grey

and cold, the Chums bored and unresponsive. In the Ghetto it
started to rain.

Dido and Nigel got off the vaporetto by the Danieli and waved
good-bye to Janet and the Chums as it swashed away. "Thank
God," she said. "Oh Nigel . . ."

"Come in and have a drink. It'll warm us up."

"Not the Danieli, Nigel darling. Please. I'd be petrified. We
could run into him or anything."

"He'll be with Manfred and his Israeli, I expect. Look, why
don't I pop inside and see? Go and get warm at Florian's. I'll
only be a minute." He had gone before she had time to argue.

Florian's was full of ghosts: a whole culture, back to Byron and
beyond, sipping and nibbling and holding forth. She sat among
mirrors and mahogany in one of the little tearooms that in two
and a half centuries had scarcely changed. Outside in St. Mark's
Square the serried tables, deprived of their string trio, endured
the rain in silence.

Why hasn't he come, she thought for the fifteenth time. She
had been there twenty minutes and a waiter was hovering. She ordered a cappuccino. Why hasn't he come? Aaronson. Muscle. Violence. Don't be a fool. Why hasn't he come?

"Nigel! Where *have* you been?"

"Having a drink with your friends. Sorry, darling. I couldn't
very well refuse. Are you warm yet? You haven't got anything—
what would you like? Irish coffee? Hot chocolate with a drop of
rum? . . . Bother the cappuccino; we'll give it to the cat.
Waiter! . . ."

Max had been expansive, and wearing dark glasses. Block had
been dignified, Aaronson alias Meyer silent. They had talked
about prices and buyer's premiums and whether Sotheby's would
get taken over. Nigel hadn't liked the way Aaronson watched
him. "I don't know what he was looking for. Now then, let's
enjoy ourselves. How to enjoy oneself in Venice on a wet Friday?
Lunch at Harry's Bar—what about that?"

"Harry's Bar? But it's *terribly* expensive! You'll be broke."

"Once in a lifetime, darling. Remember?"

"I'll go Dutch."

"No you jolly well won't. Let's go."

The Piazza was empty except for a few disconsolate pigeons.

The façade of the Procuratie Vecchie, mirrored in the sea of wet, patterned paving, made faint grey cross-rhythms with it. Her voice echoed under the arcade. "Winter's coming."

"What's it like in winter?"

"Miserable. The gloomiest place in the world, Howells called it."

"Who?"

"William Dean Howells. Nineteenth-century American. He wrote books."

"Oh. Here, give us a corner of your poncho."

There were no more arcades and a long hundred yards to go. They sprinted down the Calle Vallaresso with their arms round each other and the poncho being more of a nuisance than a help, and tumbled laughing into the bar.

It was packed, and perched bolt upright, staring at them like a startled parrot, was Elsa Silverman.

Escape was impossible. She greeted Nigel by his first name and remembered Dido from the Molo. Two drinks later it was clear they would have to be downright rude to get rid of her. It was Nigel who took the plunge. He squeezed Dido's knee and asked Elsa if she was lunching there.

She was. She was pathetically glad of their company and gradually, over the wineglasses, it came out. The trouble she'd had with Max. Not the divorce itself—it was not defended—by my *deah* the complications, and one moment he was full of generosity, and New York and São Paulo were all he wanted to keep; ten minutes later he was ranting that the split was grossly unequal and he must have Paris as well, and he'd done something to his eyes though the doctors said it was only temporary, and had trouble reading the documents, and no cheese thank you but she'd love a drop more wine, but my *deah*, at *last*, the papers were all drawn up and they were off to London to sign.

"What, both of you?" asked Dido.

"I insisted. I want my solicitor there in that room. Why should he travel half round Europe, poor man? And at my expense? It's a British company; the whole thing's under English law. London's the proper place. And there are divorce papers waiting too . . ."

"But Max . . . but I thought he had to *leave* England?"

"That's his problem. I told him. So he's finding ways and means. That's what he calls it."

Nigel squeezed Dido's knee again. "False passports or something? That'll cost him."

"My dear, very nearly. Only he doesn't need one, the way he's travelling. A day trip from Calais. He sails at crack of dawn; he'll be in London by ten and go back on the evening ferry. He'll be awfully tired, poor lamb. I mean Max, of all people, having to pig it on those ferries! His stomach won't recover for a week. Actually, it'll do him nothing but good and I hope it's blowing a hurricane. So there."

"Poor old Max," said Nigel. He made it sound very conventional. "He'll need an identity card, though. Perhaps they're easier."

"He seems to have got hold of something. He has some very strange friends."

"Tut-tut," said Nigel. "And you?"

"I'm flying to Heathrow this afternoon."

"This afternoon!" said Dido. "But Max . . . ? He stood Nigel a drink half an hour ago."

"He flies to Paris, stops in Calais overnight and there isn't a decent hotel in the place, and we're meeting at his lawyers' at eleven."

"Good Lord," said Nigel. "He's sticking his neck out, isn't he? How does he know you're not going to shop him?"

"He's just got to trust me. But I wouldn't do a thing like that, even to him. At least I don't think I would. We were very happy once, you know." She looked as if she was going to cry.

But instead she had a fit of nerves in case the plane was hijacked, and they spent half the afternoon calming her down and seeing her on board her taxi.

The rain had stopped. Autumn was staging a comeback and the whole place sparkled. On the Piazzetta a waiter distributed coffee with a flourish. They bought corn from an old woman and fed the pigeons.

"Sabotage," she said. "They're lethal. But they're so sweet. I love the sound of their little toes on the pavement. The guano holds the sulphuric acid. That's the killer."

"Acid rain."

"Rain. Smog. Mestre. Marghera. Everyone knows it. No one does anything. And the pigeons are sacred cows. I pay rates and taxes to feed them."

The two Moors on the clock tower raised their hammers and struck four. The corn was finished. "What now?" he said.

"I promised Franco I'd go and see someone. An antique shop; it's only just off St. Mark's Square. They bought some stolen things by mistake. He wants to know where they got them."

It didn't take long. Signor Abrami was happy to talk about his ivories and the dealer in Milan who sold them to him. The name Bullo meant nothing to either of them. They drifted to the Campo Santa Maria Formosa and bought persimmons from Mamma Chiara, who looked knowing. "It'll be all over the patch by now," Dido said, climbing the steps over the little *rio*. "Everyone knows everything about everybody. We're foreigners, so they'll be tolerant. It mightn't be the same if I was Italian, and if I was Venetian, heaven knows what would happen."

In the flat he waxed amorous. She said, "Business first, darling," and telephoned Scotland Yard.

Corti was out. A nice man called Billings said he wouldn't be in till tomorrow but if it was urgent he could leave word at his home and he'd call back. She said yes please and turned to Nigel, open-armed.

Afterwards, over a glass of Carpano, he kissed her and said, "You were going to spill the beans on Max?"

"It seems such a dirty trick. But he's such a dirty man." She suppressed a shudder. "I wish I knew what he'd done in England."

"Good Lord! Don't you? It was in all the papers. Selling fakes. Receiving. Then someone got killed, for grassing or something. They caught the guy and he said Max put him up to it."

"My *God!* And to think that's the man I . . . Oh my God!"

"Well, it's now or never, ducks. He won't go to England again after this."

"But Nigel, it's not fair to his wife. She'd never have told us if she'd thought we might . . . Would she?"

"Then why did she? We're law-abiding citizens, aren't we?"

"She was in a state. She had to tell someone."

"Don't you believe it. Our Elsa's had him. If she'd given a

tinker's cuss, she'd have kept her mouth shut. Public duty, darling. Spill the beans. Your Franco will love you for ever."

"I'd rather you did. Oh dear; what have I said?"

"You paid me a very pretty compliment. What's wrong with
that?"

When Corti phoned, she talked about Abrami and Bullo; then
Max and Block and Aaronson in the Danieli. Then she hung up.

"You're chicken," Nigel said. "You never told him."

"I was going to, darling, I promise. But when it came to the
point I went all weak and feeble."

"Well, if you won't, I will."

"No. I just couldn't bear it. Thinking of him in prison, going
blind. At the mill with slaves, Nigel. I don't care *what* he's done,
he's never deserved that."

"He's not going blind. It'll get better. Elsa said so. That's a rotten excuse."

It was their first row. It hadn't been too bad, they decided afterwards. He was nicer to quarrel with than Aidan. Aidan was a
jellyfish—he started off pale and shivery and barely visible and
there was nothing to hit at; then when you thought it was over,
he stung. Nigel's Anna, it seemed, had been a regular wasp's nest,
but they fought so little it hardly mattered.

By suppertime they were friends again. She thought she had
won and fed him. Then he said, "Right. What's his number?"
and went towards the phone.

This time it was worse, but in the end she gave in. "All right,
darling. You win. But look at the time! You can't ring him now!"

"Oh my God!" It was one in the morning, midnight in London. "But I must. They're on their way. If I leave it till morning,
he'll miss him. I'll just have to wake him up. He's a copper. It
won't be the first time. And don't let me forget Johnstone's
photo." Nothing would move him.

"It's out of our hands now," he said when he had finished.
"What shall we do tomorrow?"

They decided on a picnic if it was fine. There was food in the
fridge and wine in the cupboard. Vaporetto to Burano or Torcello, hire a *sandolo* and a boatman, and look for a nice wild island.

And it *was* fine and they went, and it was magic. They got seats in the bows, clear of the saloons and the scrimmage. They stood holding hands in Santa Fosca. They found a boatman who was training for the Voga Longa and was glad of a nice long row.

He stood to his oars, *alla poppa*, facing forward. She held hands with Nigel and watched, thinking, That torso belongs to the centuries. The refugees who founded Torcello came rowing like that. And it was just the same. The wild sea moor. Sanctuary.

It was half an hour before they landed. The island had been inhabited once. There were two or three acres of it, with a copse at one end, some romantic stubs of buildings, and a zigzag bank. The rest was wilderness. They went ashore at the remains of a little stone-built quay and wandered off with their food and wine, leaving the boatman to his own.

"Peace," she said.

"Not always. This must have been a fort. Come and explore that bank."

"There's old fortifications on several islands," she said. "Mussolini used them for storage. Ammunition, I think. If we'd gone much further, we'd have run up against notices saying NO ENTRY BY ORDER, THE ITALIAN NAVY."

"Oh. What have they got up there?"

"Nothing, probably. I think the notices just got left."

For a dreadful moment she wondered if the boatman had brought them where they dumped the dead of San Michele. But their island was innocent. Its ramparts had been quarried for building and only scattered blocks were left. The few ruins were beyond housing anything.

After lunch he went to sleep with his head on her stomach. She held his hand very still on her breast and thought of how his beard felt against her skin and tried to imagine living with him. Did it really have to be hell?

After a while he woke up and birdwatched through field glasses. They were sitting on the bank looking out towards the military zones across a wide stretch of water without islands. The breeze was dropping but the evening chill was early. Tonight it might turn to fog.

The only birds to be seen were gulls. "The Italians will have shot all the rest," she said.

"What on earth are those?" Contraptions of stakes and ropes were scattered in the water.

"Fish traps. Fish farming. They've done it for centuries. Hello, what's that?" Over to the right along the fringe of islands, there was a commotion among the seagulls. A few wild duck had taken off and were circling overhead. In a moment the shrill buzz of an outboard motor reached them.

Nigel pointed. A rubber dinghy had emerged from the marshland a few hundred yards away and was heading into open water. He was watching through his glasses. "Noisy devil. Hey! I know that guy! Oh. He's seen us. Damn."

Dido didn't need binoculars to see the man raise his. Suddenly she was frightened. "Who is it?"

"It's that bloody Aaronson."

CHAPTER 17

PILLAR TO POST

Waste of time, Corti said to himself. Waste of bleeding time. I must have been out of my mind.

It was half past seven in the morning. It was blowing, it was raining, and the ferry was just coming in. He hadn't even had time to notify the local law. He had left London in the dark, in a hurriedly arranged pool car, and still wasn't properly awake.

The penny hadn't dropped till he got there. It was Saturday. Whoever makes appointments at their solicitors' for a Saturday?

All right, so Elsa had travelled the day before, and her date was for eleven in the morning. But no one had said which morning or which day Max was coming, and he'd been too dopy to see it. So here he was, munching a horrible bun, drinking filth labelled coffee, and thinking what a rotten life it was, being in the job.

It would have helped if he knew what sort of travel documents Max would have, British or alien. As it was, he had to find a strategic spot in the Customs hall where everybody had to pass. He watched them straggle past with their trolleys and bags and cases, as grey and slow as convicts in an exercise yard and a great deal scruffier.

Not a sign. He waited till the ferry left on its return trip, then telephoned A & A. He got Keith Billings.

"Corti here. I'm in Dover. I want someone found and tailed. Urgent, till further notice."

Keith's voice was cheering. "Okeydoke, guv. Wilco." He wished Keith wouldn't say that.

"Mrs. Silverman. First name Elsa. Know who I mean?"

"Sure."

He gave Keith the background. ". . . Then ring the Gibbonsian and trace a Mr. Norman Johnstone, with a *t*. One of the Friends of Grinling Gibbons, just back from their Venice tour. This is urgent. If there's no one in the office, the porters must get someone. Don't take no for an answer, right?"

"Right."

"This chappie's got an exposed film with a picture on it of a geezer who could be a major villain. He was going to bring it to the Yard, after processing, I expect, and that's a month of Sundays. I want it. I want it quick. I want it processed. I want Photographic to do it, and I want the picture of two men in a speedboat on Chief Superintendent Towler's desk, Special Branch, by nine o'clock Monday morning. Right?"

"Okeydoke, guv."

"And tell them to process it nicely, or Johnstone will sue."

He set off for London. His brain was awake by now and seething. The enemy. He'd got him, unless he did something stupid like forgetting what day it was again. Elsa would lead him to him. But in case she didn't . . . He pulled up at a phone box. The gallery's number was in his notebook. He dialled.

"Good morning. Maxwell Silverman International."

"Fiona? This is Franco." He was glad it was her.

"Franco! *What* a long time! How *are* you?"

"Sleuthing away. And you?"

"Super. Really enjoying it. It's *so* much nicer." Max had really bugged her.

"I'm glad. Listen, something's come up. What time do you close today?"

"One o'clock. Why?"

"I'm coming in. I'll tell you then. I'm out of town at the moment. Half twelve, traffic permitting?"

"That'll be super."

He kept driving too fast. He couldn't help it: he was driven himself. His mind raced on. Partly it was Max and capturing him; partly it was Venice and Dido and Springer. Speedboats. The Lagoon.

Rotten job, a copper's. Having to get up at five on a Saturday morning and drive to Dover in the wet, in a car with understeer, no acceleration, and clapped-out wipers. Rotten job. Sweat your guts out for society and what does society do? Puts you under berks like Hunt. Fills your kids' minds with poison till your daughter screams "Pig!" in your face.

Franco, you're getting obsessional. You've got one of your headaches coming on. You don't want those starting up again. Or the heart trouble either. Just take things as they come. Like Max . . .

You're obsessional and you're slipping. Bombing off to Dover without checking the date! All right, maybe it was uncheckable and you'd have had to go regardless. But, Santa Maria, with your eyes open, not like this!

Fiona had been Max's receptionist. She was still very young, the eyes still starry. They were a light, clear blue with lashes as black as her hair, and very frank and open.

They kissed as friends. "I'm glad you're happy," he said. "Is she nice to work for?"

"Super. I'm not a slave now; more a partner. Not in the business sense, of course. We're both learning. She's a born businesswoman, Franco. We ought to do really well."

"I'm glad. You deserve it, both of you. Has she been in this morning?"

"She's just left. We've got it all lined up. The stationery's delivered, the sign people are coming on Tuesday. We're going to be Elsa Silverman Limited."

He nodded. "I'd heard about the split. Tuesday, eh?"

"She's signing all the papers on Monday. I think her husband's done so already. He's abroad, I expect you know."

"I do."

"Well. What was it you wanted to talk about? Oh, I see. Him."

"And her. But you've told me."

"Elsa? She's not in trouble? Franco! She *couldn't* . . ."

"Nothing like that, love. We just like to be sure what's going on. It's nice to have it confirmed by someone you can trust. Where's she doing the signing, by the way?"

"At his lawyers'. Why?"

"That's between me and him. Have you got the address?"

It was in Lincoln's Inn Fields.

It was lunchtime. He resisted the temptation to ask her out, took the car back to Lambeth, where the pool was based, and went home.

They were in the middle of lunch. On Saturdays the girls helped with the cooking, while Teresa scurried to and fro between Butter Court and Beak Street. He flopped into his chair. "*Madonna!* What a morning! A total waste of time. Not too much, darling, I've got a headache."

Sylvie came round the table and kissed his forehead. He patted her behind, smiled, held her hand for a moment. They didn't use words. Tony crashed off for paracetamol like a bull calf stung by a wasp. He winced. Teresa said, "Poor Franco. Grappa or Campari?" and gave him all the right morsels and none of the wrong ones. After lunch he went to bed.

Later, Sylvie brought him a cup of tea. He was awake and feeling better. He sat up and smiled, afraid of getting it wrong if he spoke. She sat down on the bed, and after a while said, very shyly, "It's all right, Dad. He's forgiven you."

"Wali?" he said. Cheeky young devil.

A nod. She lifted her eyes to his. He said, "Come here, pussycat," and hugged her.

"Dad."

"Yes?"

"I wish you wouldn't call me that. It's disgusting."

"Disgusting? What on earth . . . ? Good grief! You don't think it means . . . ?"

"Wali did."

"All right darling, if it bothers you." Why did she make him feel so guilty?

"Oh, Dad. Why must you be in the fuzz?"

"Somebody's got to catch villains."

"In a proper caring society there wouldn't be any."

"And how do you know that? Listen, puss—sorry. Listen, darling, reforming the world might take rather a long time . . ."

It was good to talk it through with her, but he didn't kid himself he'd changed her mind.

"Mum says policemen are always getting divorced because they're impossible to live with." The divorce rate in the Met was horrific.

"Am I impossible to live with?" he asked.

"Sometimes. Not today; at least I think not." She was smiling. He finished his tea, got up, and came downstairs.

"Franco? This is Nigel Trehoward. Dido asked me to ring; she's got a headache."

Sod it, he thought! Two calls yesterday and now on a Saturday evening. It was barely six; he'd been down for less than an hour.

"We thought you ought to know. We've just seen Aaronson out on the Lagoon. He was in a rubber dinghy. I'm afraid he spotted us. He'd got binoculars . . ."

When Nigel had finished, he said, "Listen, Nigel. I don't know if Mrs. Marsden understands quite what's happening. As I see it, there's a terrorist group, including young Springer, currently in Venice. They're Nazis—I'm not saying Germans—and they're taking part in an organised campaign of theft, destruction, and violence against Jewish art and antique dealers. We've had half a dozen incidents, both sides of the Atlantic, right?"

"You tell me. Carry on."

"Now today you've sighted an agent of Mossad, that's the Israeli secret service, who we know is associated with some of those dealers. You sighted him on the Lagoon, out beyond Torcello, right? And Springer's been seen on the Lagoon. Twice. Now none of these gentlemen wear kid gloves. And at least one of them knows, or has reason to suspect, that you or Dido or both have been taking an interest. Right?"

"Right."

"So the point I'm making is that this is getting bloody dangerous. For both of you. And if you'd allow me to give some advice, I should get that lady out of Venice, and preferably out of Italy, just as quick as you can. You can't trust the police; there's at least one terrorist sympathiser in there. Clear out, for God's sake. And do it quietly. Keep your heads down. Low profile, right? And for God's sake, keep clear of the Lagoon. Will you do that?"

"Sounds like I'll have to. It helps, you know, having the full picture. Right you are, Franco. I'll do what I can. Sorry to interrupt your weekend."

"No problem, Nigel. I'm glad you did."

Like hell he was. He called the Yard and asked for Chief Superintendent Towler's home number.

"Not on the phone, Shorty. Do you mind? Can you come round?"

"Yessir. Very good, sir." He slammed the phone down.

Damp and angry, he hammered on Towler's door. Sodding umbrella brigade! Typical! Obsessed with bloody security! Making me trail to Victoria in the wet. Pillar to bleeding post. Bloody mandarins . . . Just don't think . . . Two hours, that's all I've had with my family . . . "Oh, good evening, Mrs. Towler. Sorry to barge in at a weekend."

"Weekend?" she said, smiling. "What weekend? He hasn't heard of them. Why d'you think his first wife left him?"

He felt sorry for them both after that.

"Shorty? Come in. What are you drinking? Can't run to a Campari, I'm afraid."

"Thanks, guv. I could do with a scotch." Scotch was medicine. His headache was seeping through the paracetamol already. God, that pipe!

The scotch was a generous one. He took a good gulp, neat, and waited for Towler to settle.

"Okay, Shorty. What is it?"

"Meyer, guv, alias Aaronson. Mossad. He was seen on the Venetian Lagoon this afternoon. In a rubber dinghy, armed with binoculars. Trouble is, sir, he saw my informant, and she was with someone he'd met, and he was suspicious even then." He filled in the details, and let Towler get the names out of him. It couldn't do much harm. "I'm scared for them, guv. God knows what's going on on that Lagoon. It's where I saw Springer, if you remember, and where Dido saw him. On Thursday, I think."

"That's what you reported. With a man you thought was a big shot."

"You haven't heard the latest. You remember someone took a picture and it was stolen? Well, I've found out since, they nicked the wrong film. The right one exists, and it's in the U.K. My sergeant's tracing it now. He's to have it on your desk for Monday morning."

"I'll believe it when he does."

"It shouldn't be too hard. He could have got it already."

"Hold tight. I'll check." Towler rang his office.

"Jake? Has a camera film come in for me? That's right. From A & A. It has? Bung it round here, will you? . . . Oh. How long will that be? Okay. As soon as it's done."

He hung up and said, "Being processed. Here in half an hour. Can you wait?"

"If you think I need to." His thoughts were unprintable.

"You just might. We may not recognise Chummy, not straight away, but we'll know what he looks like. Meanwhile I'll join you in a scotch, and you can tell me how you're getting on with Dando."

It was Towler who had scrawled "Please" on Hector's bit of paper when he came looking for a job.

"Very well, guv. He's an amazing guy. Brilliant in some ways. I don't see his work, of course—I mean his work for you, or for . . . Well, I don't really know who he works for, do I?"

"That's the truth, Shorty? You really don't?"

"On my life, guv." It must be SB or MI5, but that was guess-work.

"Then you probably haven't heard. He's blown. Not his fault, but he's no good to the security services any more."

"Good God! I'd no idea! How long ago was this, then?"

"A week or two."

"But . . . What's he going to do now? I mean the Trattoria doesn't pay him. That was part of the deal, remember?"

"I was hoping you might come up with something."

"That'll be the day. Dunno, guv. There's a friend of mine down the East End runs a little security firm, but . . . Dunno. The wife won't want to lose him, but finding the money . . . I'll have to think."

"Do that. No panic till the New Year. He's still on the payroll. But after that . . ."

It was eight before he got away. The picture had come ten min-utes earlier—a clear, ten-by-eight colour print. Springer was unmistakable; so was the other man's air of command. He looked about sixty, and fit. A monocle, a duelling scar, and an Iron Cross would have suited him fine.

It would go to MI6, Towler implied, for identification. There was a time when Corti would have got all excited about MI6, but all he wanted now was his home, his paracetamol, and his bed. And a chance to think about Towler's parting shot.

"D'you fancy another trip to Venice?"

"Dunno, guv. I suppose so. Yes."

"I told you you ought to see that picture. When could you leave?"

His mind screamed, *Silverman! Monday morning! The signing!* He said, "Monday lunchtime? And that's cutting it fine."

"That ought to do. I'll talk to your guv'nor."

"Rather you than me."

"You're right," he muttered across the pillow. "It's a pig's life. Sorry it's being such a lousy weekend."

She stroked his forehead. "Must you really go on in the Met, Franco? You'll have capital. You needn't, you know. You really needn't."

"You could be right," he said. "We'll talk about it in the morning."

They didn't, of course. Fate saw to that.

CHAPTER 18

LOSERS

Because about half past eight the phone rang. The Surrey Constabulary thought he'd like to know: Wayne Little was conscious and fit for interrogation, and they wanted to get on with it before he was pumped full of dope again, so if Corti wanted to sit in could he make it for ten?

He said he'd try, swore, rang the garage, did his best to pacify Teresa, and spent the minutes till the car came perched on Sylvie's bed. He didn't stop feeling guilty till he saw the Hell's Angels.

They roared past him on the motorway in a tight wild bunch. One of them jerked two fingers upward. They were plastered with the usual insignia: death's heads, SS flashes, swastikas . . .

Swastikas with rings in the middle!

He drove the rest of the way with his brain elsewhere.

He disliked hospitals. There was something inhuman about them which seemed wrong when they were there for people. He knew they couldn't help it but you never knew if they were telling the truth, so you never dared believe them. If you were ill, you felt they owned you; if not, you made them as jumpy as they made you. He was feeling jumpy now.

It was hard to see the bandaged, screened-off body as anything but a victim. But that was villains. In custody, without their power for evil, they became human beings. At least they did for him, though for people like Hunt . . . He doubted if Hunt rated anyone as human.

Holed swastikas. It had to fit. How?

Wayne Little was a cartoonist's dream. He lay on his back with
his legs in plaster and one of them hoisted in the air. His left arm
and hand were bandaged and the left side of his face was covered
by a dressing stuck down by plaster. A lot of bruising showed
through the skinhead hair. What you could see of his face looked
awful.

"Give me ten minutes," said Chief Superintendent Fletton.
"By all means listen. After that, if you want to put any questions,
he's yours."

What questions, for Pete's sake? *It was there. It had to add up.
How?*

Fletton's personality was invisible—the sort of man you
wouldn't notice, and if you did, you couldn't give a proper description; just "medium," "average," and words like that. Perhaps
that was why he was a DCS.

He began with routine. Where the boy had been, what he'd
been doing, where he'd been going. Details of the crash itself.
Wayne swallowed his words and Fletton often had to get him to
repeat them, but the gist of it was that he'd been up the boozer
with his mates and he was that choked about his old man he
might have had one too many.

About Charlie, he stonewalled. He'd said it all before the crash.
He'd been out; he'd got back to find his father dead and filth all
over the place, and that was it. He wasn't going to budge.

When Fletton was sure of that, he nodded to Corti, and at
that exact moment Corti's mind went click and the bits fell into
place.

"You mentioned your mates," he said genially. "They'll miss
you. Skins, are they? Greasers? Hell's Angels?"

A grunt.

"Nazi gear and that?"

"Get away. That's just to take the mickey."

"There were some boys on the motorway just now. It could
have been them. They were good riders."

Wayne perked up a little. "Give 'em my love, did you?"

"Dunno if they were your lot, mind. Is there any way I could
tell?"

Wayne thought for a minute. "Yuh. Them swastika signs what

some of 'em wears. Got a sort of a hole in the middle, ain't they?"

He made himself stay friendly. "It was them then. Used to smoke a bike myself once. Nothing like it, is there? What sort was yours, then?"

"Bonneville seven-fifty."

"Terrific!" He thought he saw a spark. The bike he'd ridden himself had been a friend's two-fifty and he'd hated it, but anything for some rapport.

He took bikes as far as he knew how and switched to music and a chance to dissociate himself from Farnesford. He didn't think Wayne had actually seen him there.

"The copper as saw your dad that day said you turned the stereo on. He liked the sound. Punk, was it?"

A lot of foul language said it wasn't. It was something called "Oi." He must ask Gino about that.

He kept it up till he saw the boy tiring. Fletton, out of Wayne's sight, tapped his watch and gestured towards the ward. He'd have liked to give it longer and have the boy really exhausted, but if the hospital was going to be uptight . . .

His smile became a glare that had made seasoned coppers sweat. His voice turned bleak and hostile. "Right. Now tell me about Owen Leppard."

Wayne Little started swearing again, in a way that underlined the foulness. It reminded Corti of his Uncle Roy, and the trigger had been the same too. The name Owen Leppard.

Corti eased up. "So you know him?"

"Lepper? Sodding right, I know him. Well, I did."

"Mixed up with your lot, is he? Into swastikas and that?"

"Poxy bastard."

"You're not going to tell me he's one of yours?"

More swearing.

"More political, perhaps?"

The swearing tailed off.

"Told him about your old man, didn't you? Told him what jobs he'd done."

A ghost of a nod.

"So he leans on him. Threatens to shop him. Makes him do Pierscombe; goes along himself. Right?"

"What if he did?"

"Getting your own back, were you? Your dad got up your nose, so you did that to him. What did you do next, Wayne? I'll tell you what you did. You saw a car you thought was the law. You jumped to conclusions and ran to Chummy and started moaning that your dad was snouting. Right?"

Wayne screwed his face up in anguish.

"So Leppard did him?"

Silence.

"Put him away, Wayne. You don't have to feel bad about it. No way he's one of yours. He's not even British. It was your father, dammit."

Wayne started to cry. When he could speak, he said, "In the back, guv! In the sodding back!"

"Why should you care? You hated each other."

"He was my *dad!*" He forced the words through. "I done it, guv. I killed him. Killed my dad, didn't I, same as if I'd cut him myself."

"Come off it. How could you know he'd do that?"

"In the *back*, guv. Here—that Lepper. Not still about, is he?"

"Italy."

A long snarl out of a balloon in a comic strip. "Aaaargh! Shit! Shit! Shit . . . !" He was swearing at himself.

Out in the ward, voices protested. The sister came, armed for battle. Fletton fended her off while Corti carried on.

"Where did you think he was? Eh?"

Wayne muttered.

"What?"

Wayne pulled himself together. "How should I know?"

"Where did he live then?"

"Don't give a toss where the tosser lived, do I?"

"Oh yes you do. Come on. *Where?*" He could see the fright in the boy's eyes.

"All right, Wayne. I'll tell you. He lived at 13 Camden Terrace, and he showed you the technique. What was it? Sawdust? Detergent?" A gallon of the right mix will blister paint at two hundred yards.

Wayne's lip was trembling.

"Found your dabs there, didn't we? Fibres from the carpet on your jeans." Those were lies. There'd been no carpet left. "Come on, you might as well cough. Save yourself any more of this. You went there Monday. He was out, but his gear was there. You put that thing under his bed, set it for the middle of the night. You sprayed those signs on the wall so we'd think it was Jews; you got stoned, started home, crashed your bike, and look at you."

The boy was on the very edge. Corti fought down his pity. "But Monday evening, Chummy has it away. By the time the place goes up he's airborne. Cocked it up lovely, didn't you?"

Wayne howled like an animal. Out of the corner of his eye Corti saw Fletton holding out against the sister. It's a right pig's job, he thought. Poor little tosser. As if he wasn't suffering enough already.

He summoned his reserves and went for the knockout. *"Didn't you?"*

The boy was trying to say something between sobs. Corti bent over to listen. When at last it came it was, "So I done it. And what would you have done if it was *your* dad? Just tell me that."

Corti turned his face away. If the boy hadn't broken, he could never have gone on. He made a desperate effort to speak normally to Fletton. "You or me?"

"It's my patch. I might as well do it. Arson is it? Anything else?"

"Attempted murder. I'll fill you in later."

"That'll do for starters," said Fletton. "Wayne Little, I'm arresting you for attempted murder and arson. You're not obliged to say . . ."

Fletton was filled in. Holloway was notified. At the bedside a WPC was getting down to some serious knitting. Corti set off for home.

But the compulsion was back. There was time to call on the boy's uncle before lunch. He ought to. He owed him, for talking the way he had. Besides, he was sorry for him.

Roy was hesitant over the pavement intercom and kept him waiting in the garden, if you could call it that. Corti soon understood why. The shirt buttoned crooked under the cardy; the cigarette end smeared with lipstick; the waft of its smoke, plus gin, plus a hint of bedroom.

He pretended not to notice and accepted a scotch. "Thanks, Roy. Cheers. Sorry to barge in like this, but I think you ought to know. It wasn't young Wayne . . ."

Roy looked depressed. When Corti had finished he said, "So he'll go down. And in a few years he'll be out and that's one more villain. Mad dog, more like. It's the likes of him's giving crime a bad name, guv." It didn't sound like a joke.

"When's it had anything else?"

"Know what? I been asking myself that too. Besides, what can I do, now as Charlie's gone? I mean, who can you trust? I can't work on my own—I'd be nicked inside the hour. It was Charlie as seen to that side, see. Precautions and that."

"You'll have to turn it in, won't you?"

"Know what, guv? I just might. I been thinking about it a lot. Not short of a bob, am I? And I could make a few more if I had to, in the security business. I know more about safes and alarm systems and that than most of them what makes 'em."

"They mightn't want you, though. Not with your form."

"Form? That was twenty years ago."

"What difference would that make?" Roy's Glenlivet was doing its work and he was relaxing. "But good luck, all the same. Sometimes I think I wouldn't mind retiring too. Go into the security business myself."

"You serious?"

"Dunno. Yes. I'm thinking about it." He hadn't known how serious he was till he said that.

"Well, if you need someone what knows all there is to know about safes and that . . . No kidding, guv. Straight. And I'll go straight. I mean it. I'm sick of screwing, guv. Sick to bleeding death. I mean look what it does to you. Charlie's dead; his kids are a bleeding disaster . . ."

"Good to hear it, Roy. That's one less for us to bother about. Well, time to be going. Sorry to interrupt the homework."

"Don't get up, guv. You ought to see her. 'Ere! Louella! Come here. Give the gent a eyeful."

It was the black girl again. In her working clothes she was unnerving. He got out quick.

He made it in time for lunch, and apart from wrapping up his arrangements for the morning and Max Silverman and Venice, he got the afternoon with his family. After lunch, Wali Mohammed turned up. They were very polite to each other. Gino was tactful enough to want to stay at home, so it was safe to leave Sylvie. He took the rest to Hampstead Heath. He could feel Teresa itching to talk about the future but he wasn't ready. Instead he broke it to her about going back to Venice. She took it well. He couldn't tell her how long he'd be there; he didn't know.

Creeping into bed at night, she sighed. "Oh, Franco. When will it ever stop?"

He'd gone up early to pack, and because he would be up before five, and he only half woke up. He mumbled, "Wait till I'm back, darling. Then we'll see."

He was in Dover by seven and lurking near the British subjects' passport control with one of the port Special Branch men. Another was covering the Aliens' channel with Keith Billings. He and Keith had walkie-talkies. He'd given him Aliens because that was the one he expected Silverman to use, and Keith was the one he was less likely to recognise. There would be no trouble identifying Max. His shape and walk would show through anything.

At twenty-five past seven, Corti changed his mind. He pressed the call button of his radio. "Keith? I've decided not to take him. We'll wait till London."

"Anything you say, guv." He could imagine Keith's feelings. Organising cars, getting up in the middle of the night, flogging down to Dover, when they could have gone to Lincoln's Inn Fields in midmorning and picked him off the doorstep.

If he hadn't been so obsessive, he could have played it that way from the start. Except Max might rat. Arrive at Dover and vanish, if he came at all. Perhaps he was right to be where he was.

But suddenly he had thought of Elsa sitting in that office, with her future typed out on expensive legal stationery, wanting only her husband's signature. Wouldn't get it, would she, if he'd just been nicked?

Which was none of his business as a detective, and plenty wouldn't have given a monkey's, but . . . He should have thought of it and planned accordingly. You're getting soft, he said to himself. Soft in the heart, soft in the head. Not getting too soft for the job, are you? . . .

Then people were drifting in, and a few minutes later the radio bleeped. "He's here, guv. Grey suit. Dark glasses. Briefcase. French ID card, we think."

"Roger. Keep with him. I'll go to the car."

He sat there listening to Keith's reports.

"He's got wheels, guv. There's a chauffer. Can't see properly. I think Chummy's getting in and leaving him."

Corti called Keith in and pulled out, ready to follow. Keith's red and white clown's face was surprisingly soothing.

"There he is. Cor! Look at that!" Max was climbing into about twenty feet of BMW. "Seven-three-five! Those things'll do a ton in third! We got problems, guv. What can you get out of this, d'you reckon?"

He hadn't even noticed what make the pool car was. He grunted. "Ninety-five? A hundred?"

Can't touch him, he thought. Okay, maybe as far as the motorway, but after that . . . Question is, will he use its performance, or does he just like flash cars? Can't radio the Yard, not from here. Don't know the local frequencies. So what are the options? One, leave him right now, get on the blower and alert everything that moves. Two, follow and hope, and ring in only if you lose him. Three, don't bother; just go to Lincoln's Inn Fields and wait.

He chose option two, which could modulate into three, because he couldn't see Silverman as a fast driver, and he would be a fool to risk getting booked for speeding. Max was nobody's fool.

He was right. Max kept it legal. Corti followed a long way back. He might lose him but he wouldn't alarm him, which could mean good-bye for keeps.

The trouble began with the suburbs. Half the lorries in Europe seemed to be going their way. The traffic lights were demented, the roundabouts jammed. All you could do was follow the man in front and hope.

And suddenly the man in front was Max. There had been ten or twelve vehicles between them, and they came to a roundabout and there he was, pulling off it right in front of them.

"Jesus!" said Keith. "He went right round! Missed his road and went right round. Got some camouflage cream, guv?"

At the next set of lights, Max turned heavily in his seat, took off his dark glasses, and stared at them. At the next set but one he shot across on the red and left Corti gibbering behind a wall of buses. When it went away he was gone.

Corti said, "You drive, Keith. I'm too worked up."

They changed places to a cacophony of horns. Keith said, "Where to, m'lud?"

"What would you do?"

"No mucking about, guv. Get there."

"Me too. Get on with it."

In Lincoln's Inn Fields there wasn't a BMW to be seen. They got there at twenty to eleven. Zero hour should be eleven o'clock. Corti left Keith to park the car and did his best to look like a privet hedge. Five minutes later Keith reported in by radio and Corti posted him a hundred yards down the square.

They waited.

Nothing happened.

They went on waiting.

At five to eleven, Elsa Silverman and a fat man with a briefcase arrived in a taxi and went in.

Nothing happened for a quarter of an hour. At ten past eleven, Keith cracked a joke over the radio and got called a bleeding wally.

At a quarter past it started to rain. Corti had left his mac in the car.

At half past it was still raining and Corti was thinking about sitting by the Grand Canal in his shirtsleeves, noshing seafood and sipping Tocai.

At twenty to twelve it was raining cats and dogs and they had been there an hour.

At ten to twelve, Elsa Silverman appeared in the doorway and started flapping at taxis, but they were all full, and Corti radioed to Keith to start moving, and started moving himself, using parked cars as cover.

A minute and a half later a big man in a grey suit came out and Corti scuttled down the lines of cars bent double like a Boy Scout stalking buffalo. At the fifth car a door opened and a girl tried to stop him.

He said, "Not today, darling."

"Really! Mr. Corti! Just who do you think I am?"

"Eh?"

"WPC Terson, sir." She had changed her hairdo.

"What the devil . . . ?"

"Tailing Mrs. Silverman, sir."

He'd forgotten all about it. "She's clean. Forget her and stand by; I'm in the middle of pulling her husband. There he goes! Sodding hell, no he doesn't . . ."

It wasn't him.

Two minutes later, it was. He came out and spoke to Elsa. She turned her back.

Fifteen seconds after that, Corti arrested him and he spat in Corti's face.

Then he tried to attack Elsa, and Corti had to use his judo. Max was strong but unskilled: a simple armlock and he was helpless. Keith Billings and WPC Terson had arrived by now. Keith was brandishing handcuffs. Corti nodded to him to use them and said, "Watch out. It spits."

Max was railing at Elsa. His voice was almost unrecognisable. "This was secret! You Jezebel! You bitch! Cow! Mare! You swore on your mother's grave . . . !"

Elsa shrank, rallied, and cut in. "Shut up, damn you, and listen! I never told a soul. For God's sake, man, these are *detectives!* It's their job to know these things."

His voice recovered a little. "Not a soul? Oh, Elsa . . ."

"No. At least I don't think so. Unless . . . Oh . . . I did meet some friends in Venice, but . . . Oh Lord! Do you think I could have said something? . . ."

Max groaned. "Friends? Who, for God's sake?"

"I ran into Nigel. He was with that Marsden woman, do you remember?"

Max sat down on the doorstep with the rain driving in on him. For a moment Corti thought he was having a heart attack.

When he got up he came quietly.

Corti left him to the others and dashed home. Everyone was out. He pulled dry clothes over his shirt, which was damp but would have to do, and grabbed his suitcase. He checked in at Heathrow just as his flight was being called.

He had triumphed over his enemy. He had given Holloway their arsonist and Surrey their murderer. He felt utterly miserable and he hadn't eaten all day.

CHAPTER 19

THE *CAPOCCIA*

She had been in bed for two days with a silk scarf round her eyes. The migraine had started on the way back from their picnic, and later, when Nigel tried to take her away from Venice, it had turned into one of the worst she could remember. Her head was full of knives. The slightest sound, the slightest chink of light, and they twisted. There were others inside her stomach, set in lead. She was afraid she had said some awful things to Nigel.

It was on the way out now, and she was getting up. The routine was invariable. A brandy and soda to prime the metabolism, and by suppertime she'd be herself again. Nigel was going to cook and had gone shopping, and she was standing in her best silk undies, making her mind up what to wear.

The terror was subsiding with the migraine, but she was still afraid. Tomorrow morning they were leaving for England, via the Piazzale Roma and the airport bus, and after that . . .

After that, the way things were heading, things would be different.

"Why do you think I keep popping up in Venice?" he had said. "Once I'd recovered a bit from Anna . . . Besides, you're not safe on your own. Come on, ducks, let's give it a whirl."

She hadn't said yes at the time, because the headache was moving in, and seeing Aaronson out there with his field glasses had turned her almost catatonic with fright. But yes was what it would be. Tonight. After supper. By candlelight, with *"Che gelida manina"* or something equally soppy on the record player. "Nigel," she would say, peering deep into his soul, "are you still looking for a wife?" And he would take her in his arms, and the voices would soar, and . . .

There was someone in the flat! Footsteps were coming towards the bedroom, and they weren't Nigel's.

She dived behind the bed. The door opened.

"Get up, you silly bitch," said Shimon Meyer. He had a gun in his hand.

She shut her eyes and stayed where she was, curled up on the rug. She had seen as much as she could take. She heard his footsteps on the tiled floor, approaching.

Something thumped her bottom. His foot. She gave a little shriek.

"I said get up. You want I should drag you up by the hair?"

The kick had restarted her mind. Max hadn't been invulnerable. Perhaps this creature . . . ? The same technique . . . ? But Max hadn't carried a gun.

She sat up and dragged the counterpane over her undress. "I'm helpless, aren't I? What do you want? Money? My body?"

"Keep that for the guy who's screwing it already. If you want it to stay nice for him, you do like I say."

"For God's sake, what do you want?" She was edging towards the dressing table. The handbag with the scent spray was on top of it.

"I want to know who you're working for. Mission. Contacts. Why you're spying on us. Why you acted as you did to Max. And I haven't got a lot of time. I don't want to lose my patience, Mrs. Marsden, but if I do, God help you. Now get up. Sit here. Talk."

He propelled her to the dressing-table stool. "Now then. Answers."

It was now or never. The bag was just behind her. She grabbed. Useless. His speed was unbelievable.

He opened it with one hand. The gun in the other was horribly steady. "Silly bitch, Max warned me about that. D'you know what I'm thinking? I'm thinking maybe I play with the toy myself. Is this it? Let's see."

He squirted ammonia in the air. Her eyes began to run.

"Right, bitch. Get on with it." He stood over her, spray in one hand, gun in the other. She surrendered.

"There was this man from Scotland Yard, and he was having difficulty getting through to the right officer in the carabinieri. His contact, you'd call it. So . . ."

She tailed off. Meyer swivelled, following her eyes, to face the door. It was open, and coming through it, followed by another half-seen figure, was Franco Corti. He was pointing an automatic at Meyer and she knew at once he wouldn't have to use it. He was so obviously invincible.

He didn't even speak. Meyer put down the gun and the spray, then smiled unconvincingly at the shape behind Corti and said, "Oh, it's you. Would you mind calling your dog off, ple—"

He didn't finish. He was on the floor and his mouth was bleeding, and Corti had stopped being Superman and was swearing under his breath and sucking his knuckles. The blow had been almost invisible.

All he had known when he caught the plane was what SB had told him. They had rung the day before. Flight number. Time. Ticket and money at check-in. Briefing later. No clever stuff with passports this time, which was a relief.

And it was a relief when Towler appeared with his tie crooked and dropped things on him while he stuffed a mackintosh into the rack, leaving a sleeve hanging out. He fell into the seat beside Corti. "Crikey! Only just made it. All okay?"

"Okay, guv. A bit knackered, that's all."

"Knackered by Monday lunchtime?"

"Been up since a quarter to five, driven to Dover and back, got wet through, and haven't had a bite to eat."

"Something to show for it, I hope?"

"Oh yes. Bloke I've been after for a couple of years. Bent dealer. Fitted me up, the bastard. Nicked him a couple of hours ago. He's mixed up in this caper, by the way. Name of Silverman."

"São Paulo? Venice? The one that was seen with Meyer?"

"Right."

"We'll talk about that later. Have a kip first. You look as if you could use one."

"I could use a drink. Could you wake me up when the girl comes round?"

"I'll get you one. What would you like? Vino? Campari?"

"Scotch, guv, thanks. A big one."

He felt washed out, sour, defeated. He went to sleep.

Light woke him. They were airborne and climbing free of cloud. The plane was full of its brilliance and Towler was handing him his whisky and asking where Dido lived.

"All I've got's a phone number."

"Let's have it." Towler scribbled on a pad and reached for his bell push. A moment later two messages were on their way to the flight deck. "That ought to do the trick."

"And the other one?"

"I'll tell you when you've got something inside you."

He got out his meal tray. When he had finished, Towler said, "Right. Time to put you in the picture," and started to talk.

He began with the Brotherhood of Fatherlands and its attacks on what it called the "cosmopolitan Jewish cancer" of the art trade. The intelligence services and antiterrorist squads of the West had been interested for some years, and the most interested of all was Israel.

"Mossad," said Corti. "Meyer."

"Right. There are high-level contacts as well. They're not all formal. How many Israeli cabinet ministers can you name?"

"Begin. Sharon . . . ?"

"Any more?"

"Sorry."

"Let me give you one then. Andreas Bloch."

"Bloch? With an *h*?"

"His brother changed the spelling."

"His *brother*? So . . . ?"

"Your hot line to Israel. How did you get on to him?"

"Dunno, guv. Call it a hunch if you like." *Always play your hunches, always*, Jeremy had said. "I mean the plane. Young Jeremy holding out on me. Meyer dropping hints about Mossad. It didn't add up. A mob like that minding a few hundred thou for Block's? It had to be more than that. A lot more. So later, when I met old Block . . . He's a heavyweight, guv. I reckoned he could be the guv'nor. So I tried it on him, and the way he reacted . . ."

"Meyer's a big-mouthed oaf, and I've said so to his face."

"You mean you know him? But surely, SB . . . ? I'd have thought contacts like that were more for . . ."

Towler's voice cut hard. "That's enough. Perhaps some of us wear more than one hat. Now drop it out."

"Yessir." More than one hat. That could explain a few things. The trip to Rome two years earlier, the interest in worldwide aggro. And now this.

"And don't call me 'sir' now we're out of the U.K. Just Bill and Franco, right?"

"Bill, then. May I ask a question?"

"You may. You mightn't get an answer, but that's different."

"Just this, Bill. Why the hell are we here?"

"In my case, to build bridges, and maybe a trip on the Lagoon. In yours, to hold my hand. Interpret. Go native if you have to. Act dumb; pretend you don't talk the language; listen. In addition to that, you cover my back. Minder. Bodyguard if you like. And, arising out of that, you put the fear of God and Old Bill into Master Meyer. That lad's too uppity by half. Did you know he'd come to the U.K. against his government's specific orders?"

Corti snorted gently. "Thank God he did, or we'd all be banged up in Libya or somewhere. Carries a shooter, doesn't he? I don't know how you think I . . ."

"That's looked after. Word's gone ahead. I sent two messages, remember? Are you firearms-trained?"

"Just about scraped through. Haven't you got anyone of your own?"

"Not just like that, and not to your specification. And if you scraped through at all, you can shoot. Now leave it alone and read this. It's what decided me we should be armed."

To: DCI Corti. *From:* DS Billings.
Phone message reached A & A Saturday 1127 while was travelling Hove interview Johnstone. Begins. Urgent. Dido indisposed. At home, unable travel. Have fears for her safety. Nigel. Ends. Berkeley failed to act.

The berk! Forty-eight hours since it came in! And Keith was round the twist. "Berkeley" was his latest name for Hunt, and if Hunt saw that and latched on, he would be merciless.

He growled. About Hunt. About Meyer. About Towler. About

putting Dido Marsden at risk. About guns. About being in the job.

Outside, the world was full of shining peaks, with clouds skulking greyly in between. He turned to Towler. "Have a brandy? Or grappa, if they've got some?"

He ordered a miniature of brandy and two glasses. With them came a note for Towler, who made a satisfied grunt and passed it to him. "That's her address. Campo Santa Maria Formosa, wherever that is. And that's Chummy."

. . . Subjects of photograph: (1) confirmed K.L.O. Springer, (2) identified as Lutz Kratschsky, building contractor, resident Buenos Aires. Argentine national. Wanted for war crimes in E. and W. Germany and Poland. Former SS Hauptsturmführer. Recent recruit and potential if not actual leader, BOF. Ends.

The *capoccia*, he thought. And he wants me to tangle with that! Sod that for a lark. He grunted and said nothing.

At the airport it was colder than ten days before. It felt like ten weeks.

"Taxi. Should be waiting." Towler said when they were through the formalities.

Corti wheeled their trolley to the little dock. Three launches were moored there; theirs was the smallest. What a civilised way to travel, he thought. Civilised price, too, I bet. As they boarded their taxi a little man appeared from the direction of the buildings, waving an attaché case. "Signori, signori! Is yours, the portfolio? You left it." They'd done nothing of the sort.

Towler said, "Take it and say thank you."

"*Mille grazie*," said Corti. It was so heavy he nearly dropped it.

The taxi cast off and headed down the grass-fringed creek into the twilit street of *briccole*. They were dark and ancient and monumental, and their lights were just coming on. It had been evening last time he made the trip, with his lungs full of smog and his head of hijackers and guns. And now it was guns again but the air was clear, with clouds spread black against a washed, rusty green sky that could turn to rain. The water was choppy, and he was no sailor. He supposed the magic was still about, somewhere.

After Murano he went below. Towler pulled the cabin door to and opened the little man's case. It contained two Beretta 9-millimetre automatics, two shoulder holsters, and eight clips of ammunition. Towler slipped his holster on and grunted. "Soft-nosed, eh? Rip you up like shrapnel. Damned foreigners. Ah well. Beggars can't be choosers."

The straps on Corti's holster weren't long enough and he had to tuck the gun in his waistband. He felt a proper Charlie, and a shade seasick.

"Right," said Towler. "We'll go straight to your friend Dido. Campo Santa Maria Formosa."

CHAPTER 20

ORDEAL BY WATER

It was nice to know he could still punch, but he preferred it with gloves. Why hadn't he hit him with the gun? Plenty would have. The old bare-fist fights must have been horrific. His knuckles were oozing and Meyer's lip could need a stitch. He was sitting up and complaining to Towler through a gory handkerchief.

". . . So I put down my gun, Bill, nice and cooperative, and what does the guy do? He slugs me. Is that your British fair play?"

"Why not, in the circumstances?"

"I thought we were on the same side. My government . . ."

"Stuff your bloody government."

Corti turned to Dido Marsden, who was pulling on a kimono. "Are you all right, Dido?" It seemed funny to call her that face to face.

"All *right*? For God's sake! Don't be stupid. I'm just coming out of a migraine. I've never been so frightened in my life. I . . . Oh . . ." She clutched him and wept, and in walked Nigel Trehoward.

It was amazing how he smoothed things down. In no time he had them out of the bedroom and sitting around with the damage patched up and drinks in their hands. It was Meyer who was speaking.

"So how do I know who they're working for? The lady's poison, says Max. A police spy, he says, so I think maybe Springer's carabinieri pal Caccia. Then the guy she's going round with walks into the Danieli for no reason and takes a drink off Max and walks out again, and next thing, they're sitting on this island where no one goes, turning binoculars on me. All this I tell to Manfred, and Max is with him. So what does Max say? Find out, he says; use the frighteners; whip the bitch; chain her up in her kennel . . ."

Corti put his drink down and stood up.

He could have sworn Meyer flinched. Meyer said, "Take it easy, amigo. I only tell what he says."

"And Manfred," said Towler. "What does Manfred say?"

"Manfred don't say nothing 'cause he don't want to know."

Towler waved his Campari at him. "And how else does Silverman come into this?"

"Like the rest of them. These hoodlums been making him trouble; they been making a lot of people trouble. So Manfred rings round and says why not come and talk things over, and Venice is a nice place so he makes it Venice."

"They're all here then?"

"Some came, some didn't. Mostly they've gone home now, I guess."

It was dark but no one had bothered with the shutters and the room was lit by a single standard lamp. Dido was reclining on a chaise longue. Nigel had persuaded her into a kaftan and her colour was coming back.

Corti waited for Towler to ask the question that mattered, but he seemed in no hurry. Finally he asked it himself.

"What were you doing on the Lagoon, Mr. Meyer?"

"Finding out where these guys go and what they do there."

"And did you?"

"They come and go a lot. There's islands right at the end. Torcello's about halfway. I say islands but that's not right; you want to look at a map. There's a place where they're continuous in one piece right across the Lagoon. You couldn't get a boat through. And after that they go on for four or five kilometres before you get to the end. You go out there, you get these 'no entry' signs, so me, I keep out. I don't know what these guys have got out there but they've got something. Maybe there's a channel some place that isn't on the charts. Maybe they cut one—there's necks of land only a few metres across—because their boats disappear where they ain't no call to disappear. Me, I ain't been no further than Lio Maggiore, and that's pushing it. Guess I'm running kinda scared. Twice now they see me out there. Last time they come to take a closer look."

"They," said Towler. "Who's they?"

"Number One. Number Three. Maybe a soldier or two. I got pictures but no names. Jerusalem could have some; I wouldn't know. The only name I got's their Number Two. Him I ain't seen." `

Towler said, "I'll trade. Three's called Springer. You can have the rest when you've given me Two."

Number Two was an Argentinian called Diego Sánchez O'Hagan who'd been a naval captain till he got in bad with the junta. Though that, Meyer said, could be cover. Number Four, he volunteered, was a Libyan, and through him every kind of horror could open up. Mossad hadn't got hard evidence but feared ties with the Middle East. PLO or worse. When you got that near the edge, left, right, what did it matter? Look at Hitler and Stalin in '39. Jerusalem got kinda neurotic about that angle.

"Don't blame them," said Towler. "Where do we go from here? The Italians won't move."

"If I had someone with me—a guy who'd be some use if we got into trouble . . . Maybe we could go on past Lio Maggiore a little."

Towler's Campari indicated Corti. "He can look after himself. You've been on the receiving end."

It would be light in two hours and he was very angry. It was his second morning in Venice. The anger and the sense of unreality went together. The deeper parts of his brain hadn't caught up. Perhaps the anger was why. He had gone through the preparations in a kind of daze. They had had a job getting clothes. The sweater was easy but all the waterproofs they could find were plastic and too conspicuous. They settled at last for orange overtrousers and a dark canvas blouse that was only splashproof.

He resented it. He was sure Towler had had something like this in mind from the start, and he resented being conned. He resented getting up in the middle of the night. He resented being in someone else's war and having to work with Meyer. He resented open boats on principle. He resented whatever macho thing it was that had stopped him refusing. He wasn't frightened yet but he knew he would be. He resented that too.

He sat glowering on an overinflated cushion while Meyer, looking like a poor man's Spencer Tracy in a long black oilskin, started the motor and waved to the man in the boatyard and headed into the dark. He resented the noise the thing made. The clips of ammunition in his pockets were heavy and inaccessible and the strap of his shoulder holster, extended by string, was chafing already.

He asked Meyer, "Are you a sailor?"

"Why? Are you?"

"Me? You're joking."

"Join the club, amigo," said Meyer.

The night was cold and still and shrouded in grey felt. Somewhere above there would be a moon. The sluggish Lagoon tide was low and should rise, when it did, no more than three feet. To the left, the chain of sodium lanterns looped away to Murano lighthouse, flashing, steady, off, on, steady, off, on. Ahead, the clouds reflected flashes in other rhythms. A pattern of lights moved slowly across and boomed. It made him jump. He thought of Teresa, warm and comfortable in bed, and suppressed a growl.

Meyer headed east along the northern quays, skirted the docks beyond the Arsenal and swung left. Soon they were crossing the Lido entrance to the Lagoon, and the boat rocked to a lazy swell. They passed a lighthouse syncopating white above with green below; two others flanked the channel to seaward, and between and beyond them, smaller, coloured lights twinkled on and off. Here and there there were sandbanks. It was very beautiful, very mysterious.

Soon they bore left again. "Treporti channel," said Meyer. Corti had lost his sense of direction. To the right the land was inhabited; to the left, all you could see was *briccole*. An hour after they pushed off they were in a wide, desolate creek with not a house and hardly a tree to be seen. Meyer said Torcello was five kilometres to the left. Corti was cold. He felt thin beginnings of fear.

After that it was creeks and channels with land always to the right and either land or mudbanks to the left. They passed a notice board. Lit by Meyer's torch, it said ACCESS FORBIDDEN and needed maintenance. "Too bad," grunted Meyer. Twenty minutes later he grunted, "Lio Maggiore." All Corti could see was a few trees half a mile to the right. Not long after, the marsh receded. Meyer got out a compass.

"Channel don't seem to be marked. Let's hope there's enough water. This thing don't draw a lot, and the tide's coming in." Corti hoped he knew what he was doing. He slipped a hand under his waterproof to make sure of the Beretta.

They were going slowly now. Corti was uneasy about the noise, but the thought of oars was daunting. Besides, as Meyer said, if there was anyone around they'd be seen regardless, and they hadn't got all day. The whole point was to be gone before anyone came.

Very soon there was land again. The sky was lighter. He could see an apron of mud and a low tussocked crest. And the straight, clean channel gouged through both.

Meyer muttered, "Geronimo," and took them in.

It was hardly more than a ditch. Fifty yards and they were through into a marsh-fringed mere. A little to the left, a long silhouette of wall stood out of the land.

Meyer cut the engine. Corti rowed. He was no oarsman. The oars were fixed to pivots or he'd have lost them three times over. Five minutes and much whispered bad language later they tied up at a little landing stage. Some of the planks were new.

Corti whispered, "Better get these oilskins off. They'll make a noise." It took a surprising amount of effort: he hadn't known quite how cold and stiff he was. He could get at his ammunition now. Meyer refuelled the engine from a jerrican and they went ashore, guns at the ready. Corti decided it was only the cold that was making him shiver. A small, sparse drizzle filled the air.

It didn't take long to establish that the building was an old fort and lay on an island. Either it had worn extremely well or it had been restored. The walls were of brick and stone and set on an embankment. Every so often there were embrasures for cannon. There was no sign of life. He began to feel quite brave.

Inside, the ground was eight or ten feet below gun level and on it were several buildings. One must have been a barracks and was built of brick, with stucco falling off and a tiled roof. The others looked like superannuated army huts.

The locks were easy. In the huts there was only litter, except for some empty storage racks in one. The larger building was more complex. It had two stories, the upper one disused, the lower divided into rooms. In the first of these there were stacks of crates labelled agricultural machinery. Meyer opened one. It was full of machine pistols.

Next door they found tins of food, in another room two camp beds, in the next, rudimentary eating and living facilities. The pin-ups on the walls were hard sadistic porn, and largely homosexual.

The last room was the office and decorated with framed photographs. One was of Mussolini. In another, a young man in a black uniform was having a medal pinned on by Hitler. The third was of Lutz Kratschsky wearing a similar medal but on a different uniform. It had holed swastikas on the lapels.

The office equipment was mostly two small locked metal cabinets. They opened easily to Corti's jigglers. They were full of microfiche.

The viewer was on the table. He switched it on but nothing happened. Meyer said, "There'll be a generator some place."

"There'll be time for that later."

"Too right, amigo. We've seen all we need. Let's go."

Outside, the drizzle had turned to rain and a breeze was stirring. It would be chilly heading into it. Corti envied Meyer's oilskins.

The mud flats were covered already. The rain was falling through mist and you couldn't see far. Meyer got out his compass. "We'll go for Torcello. Straight across—maybe nine kilometres. Should be enough water for us but not for them. They'll have to go round, so we shouldn't meet them."

He felt seasick after five minutes. After ten they were out of sight of land. It was nasty against the wind, with rain in his face and the seas kicking beneath. They were short and choppy and getting bigger. He was foully uncomfortable. His canvas blouse was sodden, he'd got spray down his neck, and he was frightened: not of Springer and his Hauptsturmführer so much as of the sea and the loneliness and Meyer, whom he didn't trust an inch. He had visions of engine trouble, of capsizing, of a sudden knife. Or a heel in the throat that would put him over the side. He remembered Charlie Little, chucked like rubbish on a tip behind the pot plants. He remembered his face. He remembered his own father's.

He shivered. He could never react fast enough; he was far too stiff. He felt sick and chilled to the bone and his bladder was complaining. He kept his hand on the holstered gun.

Then the fish ranches began. Stakes. Long screens of wattle, pushing them off course. Fenced-off clusters of piles and ropes, shaggy with mussels. Sudden currents. Turbulences, as if there were submerged weirs. The voyage became an obstacle race. They ran aground twice. Once, their screw fouled a net and neither of them had a knife and they had to tip the engine inboard and kneel to clear it at arm's length, with the dinghy tossing and each in turn sitting on the other's feet to make a counterweight. It was agonising and wet and numbed their fingers. It took twenty minutes.

Navigation was a farce. The whole thing was a farce. That Meyer was a clown and downright dangerous. Towler must be out of his mind, entrusting him to that. He hated them both.

They jarred on through grey cold loneliness. It got a little easier as the tide rose. He wished he could be sick. After, he didn't know when the seas stopped getting bigger. Meyer said, "Not far now." Soon a line of reeds appeared, thrashing in the wind.

"No way this is Torcello," said Meyer. "Left, I guess." After a while the reeds gave way to vines. Soon there were *briccole*. They followed gratefully.

Then the speedboat appeared.

It loomed from the murk a quarter of a mile ahead and changed course towards them. Head on, it looked the size of a destroyer. Even through the snarl of the outboard Corti could hear its engines open up. Its bow rose. It spread great wings of spray and flew straight at them.

Meyer said something foreign and put the helm over hard, and Corti nearly went over the side. For a moment they were head on and he thought Meyer had gone mad and they'd had it. But at the last moment he swung away. The bow wave soused them and nearly tipped them overboard. Poised momentarily on top of it, Corti glimpsed Lutz Kratschsky. He was loading a revolver.

Corti shouted to Meyer, "What happens if we're punctured?"

"We lose a watertight compartment. We got three. He's faster than we are." The news did him no good at all.

The launch came again, and again Meyer faced it and sheered off at the last moment. This time he went the other way and Corti only saw Kratschsky's back.

The third time it came slower, and Kratschsky was aiming at them from the bows. Meyer faced them again and swung off when he was fifty yards short, relying on his smaller turning circle. Through the din of wind and engines and slapping seas, the pistols in the speedboat sounded harmless as toys.

But something not at all harmless whirred past Corti's head. A ricochet off the water. A bullet flying wild like that, tumbling end over end, wouldn't drill wood tidily but would splinter and smash. He fired back, aiming low, using the sense-of-direction method. Two rounds, bang-bang, as quick as he could pull the trigger. Meyer only managed one, but it hardly mattered. At that range from the bucking dinghy the chances of a hit were minute.

The speedboat came many times, trying to ram or shoot or both. It was over twenty feet long, decked in forward with an open cockpit, and it could go like the clappers. Springer was at the wheel, while Kratschsky did most of the shooting. Thank God it was only handguns. And thank God for the rubber dinghy. The way the waves were throwing them about; they must be an impossible target.

Meyer had been steering with one hand and shooting with the other. He was reloading now, with the tiller under his arm. Corti was into his third clip of ammunition and they seemed to have slowed the launch down. It was coming at them once again. And this time it anticipated Meyer's swerve and Corti got a close-up. There was a ragged hole under its bows as big as a 10p piece. He put two more near it.

They were going to pass close. Meyer yelled, "Take a man!"

He didn't need telling. He got his two rounds off as the speedboat passed astern. The second one felt right.

He saw Springer stagger and the launch veer. He saw Kratschsky fire. Twice, he thought. The dinghy went sluggish and lopsided. Meyer was leaning heavily against the side, and the side was deflating.

He said, "Meyer! Are you all right?"

Meyer didn't seem to hear. He was sinking into the punctured tube, lying almost flat, with his shoulder in a pool of water. The floorboards were tilting, and each time a wave came he slipped a little. Corti grabbed an ankle.

Meyer started kicking. He had let go of the controls and the dinghy was wallowing in circles, and Corti had to keep an eye on the speedboat. It was all over the place. At one moment it was pointing away from him and he saw Springer clinging to the wheel and fighting off Kratschsky who was trying to take over.

Then Meyer kicked Corti's gun hand and hurt it and he dropped the gun, and he couldn't hold on any longer, and Meyer slid away, leaving blood behind him, and at last Corti was sick.

And the speedboat was coming again and there was a *briccola* and the dinghy was out of control, and . . .

The two boats hit the *briccola* together.

The dinghy went over sideways till the bottom was above him, and the last thing he saw was CARABIN-something painted white on navy blue, very bold and plain. He didn't believe it.

CHAPTER 21

ALLA SALUTE

The mud caught him in great sucking mouths. They thrust tongues between his teeth. They gulped down hands, forearms, elbows. All round him there were timbers. Above, in another world, the waves were beating his legs against them.

He concentrated on his right arm, but his only purchase was against the mud, and the more he tugged the deeper he burrowed. By the time he got it free his left shoulder was in, but he could twist his face clear and start unblocking his mouth.

The left arm wouldn't budge. His mind was very cold, thinking out ways to free it. If he could get his body horizontal . . . But the timbers stopped that. Must be the *briccola* . . .

The Lagoon flooding into his lungs was cold as death.

He was in a narrow passage like a Venetian *calle*, walking towards the light. At the end of it there was a small river with grassy banks. It was early summer. The turf was springy and jewelled with flowers. The air was full of birdsong and everywhere there were butterflies. A dragonfly hovered and flicked away.

On the far bank there were people. They looked young and happy. Some were talking and laughing. A few waved to him. He wondered if he would see someone he knew. A woman was calling.

"Franchino! *Bambino mio!*"

He knew the voice instantly after thirty-five years. There she was, tall and brave and young; more beautiful than he remembered.

"Mamma!" he called *"Mammina!"*

"Come across, Franchino."

"Come across," called his father, no longer a potbellied stubble-headed old git but sturdy, with a mop of dark hair.

Shall I? he asked himself. You can't get back. Do I need to? *Madonna della salute*—my Lady of Salvation. Help me to choose.

The crowd parted and knelt for her. It was not at all dreamlike but perfectly natural. He got down on his knees and crossed himself. She stood on the far bank and smiled to him. Her face was dark and fine. Many delicate gold chains hung across her breast. Her voice was the sweetest he had ever heard. "I cannot choose, Franco. You must do that yourself. Don't be afraid. You are loved in both earth and heaven. You are a man, Franco. Choose."

She was as real as Teresa. Or Sylvie. And so like her. Sylvie, with her first boy . . .

Sylvie needed him.

"*Madonna*," he said. "*Madonna fosca*. I have chosen. I do not think it is time. Not yet. I haven't finished at home."

She smiled and raised her hand in blessing. He crossed himself again. When she had gone he turned away.

After that there was a moment when he hovered above grey water looking down at a wooden pylon. A launch was moored to it and a smaller one was lying on its side, half submerged. A rubber dinghy with one side collapsed was floating away upside down, with a man in a boat rowing after it.

Two men in sodden clothes lay on the launch's deck. He couldn't tell if they were alive. Others, in peaked caps and oilskins, were dragging something from beneath the pylon and laying it beside them. One of them knelt and started thumping it rhythmically. Another attended to its head.

He felt fingers exploring his throat. Water flowing out. Lips on his own, blessedly warm. Warmth blown into his chest. The thumping.

He rested for a minute or two, then opened his eyes.

"Thank God," said Bill Towler.

"*Grazie al cielo!*" said Giorgio Montani.

"Meyer?" he said when he could speak. He was below, lying across the launch on a bench seat, weighed down with coats and oilskins.

Giorgio shook his head. He looked tired. Towler wasn't there.

"Have they found him?"

"Not yet. I shouldn't try to talk."

"Then those two on deck?"

"Opposition."

"Alive?"

"The *capoccia*. A wetting and a knock on the head. He'll live. He's behind you."

"Not Springer?"

"Dead."

"Drowned? Or did I . . . ?"

"Who knows? He was hit in the side. We have no postmortem facilities on board."

The motion of the launch was changing, and the engines were opening up.

"Meyer then?"

"No point hanging about. They would have found him if he had surfaced. We must get you to the hospital."

"*Madonna*," he said. "Do you have to?" He shouldn't have said "*madonna*" like that.

"Of course. You could get pneumonia."

He rested a little, then said, "You weren't long in the Mezzogiorno. What happened?"

"You remember Major Caccia? Dido saw that son of a whore going into his house?"

"Yes."

"I had been able to get the information to the right quarter. There could be a court martial, and the major is removed from his post. It is mine now. You may congratulate me on my promotion."

"Great," he said and closed his eyes.

Springer dead, Meyer dead. He'd never fired in anger before, let alone killed. Because whether it was the bullet or the Lagoon, Springer would be alive if he hadn't hit him. It didn't seem to matter a lot, though he was sorry about Meyer.

"Giorgio," he said.

"He's outside. It's Bill."

He opened his eyes. "I didn't hear you come in."

"You dropped off. How are you doing?"

"Cold. Otherwise okay. Bill—how did you get here?"

"Ah. I thought I'd take a shufti at Mr. Caccia; rang in, asked to call. Chief Super and all that. They said he wasn't around but Major Montani would be happy to oblige. So we had a word. In French. I told him what was up; he said to come round straight away and the launch was waiting. He knew where Springer and Co. kept their boat from before he was posted away, so he laid on a tail. His man was just in time to see them cast off. We were afraid they might run into you so we followed at long range. Radar. Closed up when they started circling. Heard shots, moved in. Bob's your uncle."

"Great. Saved my life and that. Thanks."

"And you. Did you find anything?"

"Bit tired . . . Yes. Tell you later . . ." Let him sweat, he thought. So he saved my neck. And who put it on the flaming block? Didn't save Meyer's, did he? Bloody hospital . . .

They let him out in the morning with a clean bill of health. He went straight to the Salute to pay his respects to the Madonna and light her a candle. In the afternoon Giorgio took him and Towler looking for fascist hideouts in a helicopter. Visibility was poor and it took time, but he found it for them, and they picked up a crate or two of guns and all the microfiche.

Next morning he and Towler flew home. Dido was on the plane, with an enormous bouquet Giorgio had brought when he came to pay her phone bill. She'd got Nigel with her. Over the Alps they said they'd got engaged and produced champagne.

He took a glass from politeness. After a while it got through to him that she was leaving Venice. He said, "Won't you be sad?"

"Of course I will. I adore the place. But on balance I'd as soon have him."

"Venice is dead," said Nigel. "She's a ghost. She's been one since Napoleon and she'd been sick for centuries before. Oh, she's gorgeous and romantic and full of nostalgia, but that's not life. Why do you think she gets on the Venetians' nerves? She's death, Franco. That's why. Death to anyone who wants to *do*. She'd have been death to Dido. Wouldn't she, darling?"

"I don't know. Yes. She does get hold of you. She was turning me into a bookworm. Poor Venice. I do love her so."

"When I think what's being poured in there," said Nigel.

"Technology, money, skill. And when I think what else she'll need to keep her going . . . Going, not alive. Just walking dead. All this shoring up the past and then kowtowing to it's downright unhealthy. The past's over. It's given us all it can. Let it be."

"Wouldn't it be awful if he's right? Perhaps he is. It's all so sad."

"Don't worry, darling. I love the old trollop, just like the rest of us. I fund-raise for Venice in Peril with the best of them." Nigel raised his glass and declaimed,

> "Men are we, and must grieve when even the shade
> Of that which once was great is pass'd away.

Wordsworth. That's about Venice and he wrote it two hundred years ago. Of course it's sad. What does Franco think?"

"Me? It's no use asking me. I'm a Florentine."

"There speaks a survivor," said Nigel.

"There speaks Italy," said Dido.

"Same thing," said Corti.

That night at home it caught up with him. The family left him in peace. He was beginning to recognise their techniques for Dad's moods. He went to bed early, and was surprised when Gino followed him upstairs.

"Was it rough, Dad?"

"You could call it that."

"You're different. Something's happened. You haven't told us, have you?"

How do you tell your children that you've killed a man, you've been to the edge yourself and talked with Our Lady? That you only chose life because of them?

"Not tonight, Gino. Tomorrow maybe."

"Dad . . . Are you really leaving the Met? Mum said . . ."

"I might. I haven't made my mind up." One good thing about Venice was that he hadn't had time to worry about that. It wasn't a decision to rush. He'd done twenty-three years. Two more and he'd get half his pension.

In the morning he opened Zappaterra's envelope and it told him of another Venetian Jewish dealer who'd had trouble with stolen goods. A bit late for that, he thought, but bully for Zapp. And there was a letter from Bennett saying that probate was finally through and the property and the pictures were his. There was also a message to contact Hector Dando. He went round to the Trattoria Vaccarino.

"Chief Inspector! You are well?"

"Not too bad, considering. Lucky to be alive actually. I damned near got drowned. Have you ever had to use a gun?"

For a second, emotions seethed visibly behind Hector's pallor. Then he smiled, with a vague dismissive gesture and said, "*Prego* —do you mind?" Anyone else would have asked questions.

"Bill tells me you're out of it."

"That is correct, Chief Inspector."

"Listen—if I were to pull out as well—set up on my own— investigations—security. Only if, mind you. Would you be interested in joining me?"

"I am totally at your disposition." Over the moon, his face said.

"I'm glad. No promise, mind, but don't take another job without talking to me first. Now. You wanted to see me?"

"Bullo, sir. Is active member of MSI. Movimento Sociale Italiano. You know MSI? The big fascist party? Is arrested for receiving stolen things."

"That's great, Hector. You promised it in a week, didn't you? It's exactly a week today. I like that."

"Thank you. And your other question—an officer in the carabinieri in Venice. I am told that a certain Major Montani could be sympathetic."

"He could. What's more, he saved my life."

At the Yard, photographs of swastikas collected by Interpol were waiting for him. The styles were varied but they all had holes in the middle. Might as well dot the i's, he thought. He summarised his information, including Zappaterra's and telexed it to Giorgio in Italian, officer to officer, with a translation plus the news about Bullo for Towler, and official confirmation, according to the rules, through Interpol. "Sodding bureaucracy," he muttered and answered the phone.

It was Towler. "Thought you'd like to know, Shorty. They've started on the microfiche. They've got enough already to roll up the Brotherhood of Fatherlands for keeps. If the Argies play ball. But that's their problem. It's this side of the Atlantic that's ours."

"What is it then? Their central records or something? Where's their HQ?"

"Buenos Aires. But Kratschsky's German trained. He's efficient, so he's had it all microfilmed and duplicated to HQ Europe for safekeeping."

"Where's HQ Europe then?"

"Short of Venice, I wouldn't know just yet."

"Well, thanks for ringing, Bill."

"Not Bill, do you mind? Not in the U.K. I've spoken to you about that before."

He managed to say, "Sorry, sir," before hanging up, and at that moment in waltzed Keith Billings. He snapped, "Yes?"

Keith pulled himself up short. "Oh. Sorry, sir. I was going to ask if you'd heard about the Guv."

"What about him?"

"Had a stroke. Not too bad, it seems, but he won't be coming back."

"Hmph. Pity." He was a bully, he was thinking, but he was a good copper and he looked after me when I was in trouble. Better the devil you know . . . "Have you heard who we're getting?"

"Hunt." He didn't even say "Mr."

When Billings had gone he sat at his desk for a minute, staring at nothing. At least you could respect the Guv. But Hunt . . . Two years of that for half a pension? "Join me in the business," his father had said. "You could throw your salary in the Thames and never notice." If he could have stayed with the Silverman job, it might have been different, but with offences against himself on the charge-sheet that was impossible. Oh, to hell with Silverman.

He was feeling slightly nostalgic already when he stumped through the Squad's busy office to the stationery cupboard. There was a form for everything.

Next day, the new fascia said ELSA SILVERMAN in silver Art Deco lettering. Quite nice, he thought, striding past towards Butter Court. A little on the brash side for Duke Street, but why not? He was developing a fellow feeling for Elsa.

It was Friday, so it wouldn't matter if the children stayed up late. He had said nothing to the family except that they were booked in, all three generations, at the Trattoria. He had briefed Hector about the drinks and personally put the second chef on his mettle, and Teresa had promised faithfully not to keep running to the kitchen.

He sat between Sylvie and Teresa's mother. Towards the end of the meal he raised his voice to take in the whole table and told them about Venice and Springer and Meyer and the holed swastikas, and the microfiche and the fight on the Lagoon. Out of the corner of his eye he saw Hector lurking within earshot. That was okay by him.

He went on to his visions. "You can say it was a dream, and perhaps it was. Personally I think it wasn't, but at the end, who can say?"

They were silent. He was one with them. He could feel their love as an almost physical glow, and it wasn't just the Chianti.

"It wouldn't be right to drink Our Lady's health. But we can drink to what she brings us." He stood up. "My dearest family, the best of all toasts. *Alla salute!*"

When he had sat down, he said to Sylvie, "They were fascists, you know. Real ones. How do you stop people like that without the fuzz?"

She blushed and simpered and he knew it was all right.

He stood up again and rapped the table. "And I have another toast. Come on, Hector. You're in on this. Fill up. We all know some of you would like me to leave the police. Well, never say I don't listen. End of next month. No, wait for it . . ."

He was having trouble with his voice.

". . . So let us drink to our future, to our new enterprise. I give you Corti & Co. *Salute.*"

ABOUT THE AUTHOR

In his varied career, Peter Inchbald has been an army officer, an art student, a professional painter, a cutlery and silverware manufacturer, a consultant in design management, a conservation society secretary and chairman, and a sculptor. SHORT BREAK IN VENICE completes the trilogy which began with *Tondo for Short* and *The Sweet Short Grass*, all published by the Crime Club. He and his wife make their home in the English countryside.